Amelia's
SUMMER SURVIVAL GUIDE

by Marissa Moss

(and all-set-for-summer Amelia)

FEATURING

Amelia's	**Amelia's**
LONGEST, BIGGEST, MOST-FIGHTS-EVER FAMILY REUNION	ITCHY-TWITCHY, LOVEY-DOVEY SUMMER AT CAMP MOSQUITO

2 SUMMERS IN 1!

SIMON & SCHUSTER BOOKS FOR YOUNG READERS
NEW YORK   LONDON   TORONTO   SYDNEY

Kathleen Caldwell,
wishing her the best summer ever!

SIMON & SCHUSTER BOOKS FOR YOUNG READERS
An imprint of Simon & Schuster Children's Publishing Division
1230 Avenue of the Americas, New York, New York 10020

Amelia's Longest, Biggest, Most-Fights-ever Family Reunion
Copyright © 2006 by Marissa Moss
Amelia's Itchy-Twitchy, Lovey-Dovey Summer at Camp Mosquito
Copyright © 2008 by Marissa Moss

SIMON & SCHUSTER BOOKS FOR YOUNG READERS
is a trademark of Simon & Schuster, Inc.
Amelia® and the notebook design are
registered trademarks of Marissa Moss.

For information about special discounts for bulk purchases, please contact Simon & Schuster
Special Sales at 1-866-506-1949 or business@simonandschuster.com.

The Simon & Schuster Speakers Bureau can bring authors to your live event. For more
information or to book an event, contact the Simon & Schuster Speakers Bureau at
1-866-248-3049 or visit our website at www.simonspeakers.com.

A Paula Wiseman Book

Book design by Amelia
(with help from Tom Daly)

No fonts
or
typefaces → The text for this book is hand-lettered.
were harmed   Manufactured in China
in making   0311 SCP
this
book!   2 4 6 8 10 9 7 5 3

CIP data for this book is available from
the Library of Congress.

ISBN 978-1-4424-2331-2

These titles were previously published individually

Amelia's

LONGEST, BIGGEST, MOST-FIGHTS-EVER FAMILY REUNION

by Marissa Moss

(and daughter, sister, half-sister, niece, cousin, stepdaughter, granddaughter Amelia!)

Simon & Schuster Books for Young Readers

New York   London   Toronto   Sydney

That's what my dad was for most of my life — a big fat question mark. All I knew about him was that he left when Cleo, my sister, was two and I was just a baby. Mom must have been really mad at him because she never told us ANYTHING about him. It was like he didn't even exist. Or maybe we didn't exist for him. I mean, if he wanted to find us, he could have figured out a way. But he didn't.

I was the one who finally found him. I nagged and super-nagged Mom until she gave me his name and address. I was excited to see he actually lived somewhere besides my imagination, but I was also FURIOUS at Mom. She knew where he was ALL ALONG — she just wouldn't tell me or Cleo.

Mom

I don't know why you want to write to him. He's never written to you.

All you've ever gotten from him was your name. He picked out Amelia for Amelia Earhart. Don't expect anything or you'll be disappointed.

Maybe he DID write to me, but Mom never gave me his letters. How would I know?

I'm just saying...

Just because she hates my dad doesn't mean I have to.

So I wrote him a letter — actually, a comic strip — telling him I was wondering who he was and why he went away. That was hard, but even harder was waiting for him to answer. Part of me was afraid he wouldn't, part of me was afraid he'd tell me to leave him alone, and a teeny, tiny part of me was hoping he'd tell me how much he loved and missed me.

He didn't do any of those things. When I finally got a letter back, he said he was sorry and wanted to be in my life and he invited me to visit him in Chicago, where he lives. But he didn't say he loved me. He just signed the letter "Dad."

What could I do? I went to Chicago. That was last year. I've seen him a couple of times since then and we e-mail and talk on the phone. I know he's trying to be a good dad, and I'm not mad at him anymore, but I still think he should have been there when I was little. He could have tried. So could have Mom. They both say they have their reasons, but I think they're lame excuses.

Dad's version

Amelia, I'll be honest with you — it was a painful divorce. I needed to travel for my work as a reporter and I couldn't be with your mother as much as she needed. We fought about it for years, long before you were born. We kept hoping things would get better, but they didn't. Once we finally decided to separate, neither of us wanted to see the other one. It was pretty ugly. You and Cleo were both so young, I thought it would be easier if you never knew me.

When we first met in Chicago, he was really nervous. So was I. I didn't know what to expect, what kind of dad he would be, and what it would feel like to call someone "Dad."

Easier on who, I wondered — him or us?

Even though he'd remarried and had a baby, my half-brother, George, he didn't know how to be a dad to _me_. When he picked me up from the airport, he brought me a teddy bear, like I was a baby or something. NOT what you give an 11-year-old girl. I gave it to George. He liked it. →

He didn't give me what I really wanted — a hug. But we're both better at that stuff now. He tells me he loves me and hugs me. He's better at teasing me and getting my sense of humor. He still has awful taste in clothes when he buys me stuff, but he's learning. And he's told me more about why he left and why he didn't try to see us. Part of it was for our sake, part of it was because Mom was _really_ mad at him.

Mom's version ↓

It was a BIG mistake right from the beginning, but I kept on trying, I really did.

We were seeing a counselor, trying to work things out when you were born. But it all got worse, not better. Quentin wanted out and out he went. I was so ANGRY, I couldn't stand the sound of his voice. I wanted no contact — NONE!

When Mom first told me this, it made me feel terrible, like it was my fault they got divorced. Maybe they could have stayed together if they'd only had one kid to handle. Then I got mad at Mom. Maybe Dad would have helped if she'd let him. I mean, was that fair to Cleo and me?

Anyway, Carly, my best friend, says no one can understand what goes on in a marriage — the good and the bad — except the people in it. Her parents aren't divorced. They have a really good marriage (at least it looks that way to me, on the outside), but her mom is an expert on broken marriages because that's her job, marriage counseling. (She calls it couples therapy, but it's the same thing.) When I told Ms. Tremain about meeting my dad for the first time (that I can remember), she had some great advice.

Amelia, you need to build your _own_ relationship with your dad based on _your_ experiences with him, not on what your mom says.

Even after all these years, your mom still has a lot of anger and resentment. Without realizing it, she may say things to sabotage your relationship with your dad. That kind of thing can happen.

She also said there was no point in blaming either of them for the past. The question was, what kind of future did I want to have with them? I still can't help being angry about it all, but I'm trying to think about what I want _now_. That's hard-enough work!

Ever since my visit, my dad's been figuring out how to get me back into his life. I'm figuring out _if_ I want to be there.

It's a lot to get used to! There's not just Dad, there's his second wife, Clara, not my favorite person in the world, and their baby, George (who, I admit, is one of my favorite people — he's so adorable!). And there's all the family attached to them — aunts, uncles, cousins, grandparents — all of them to consider.

For most of my life, I had a very small family — just me, Cleo, and Mom. When we went to family gatherings, it was still pretty small.

Cleo
↓

↑
She takes up a LOT of space even if she's just one person. She's LOUD and BOSSY and PUSHY.

Mom
↓

↑
She's mostly quiet, not the chattiest person, but once she starts lecturing — WATCH OUT!

Me
↓

↑
I'm the creative spark of the family. Without me, things would be totally out of balance.

↑
Aunt Lucy — she's the opposite of Mom in every way. Mom's super-organized and controlled. Lucy always forgets basic stuff — like packing a toothbrush or leaving the oven on.

↑
Raisa — she's the little girl Aunt Lucy adopted from Russia when she was 3. Now she's 5 and her English is pretty good but she's shy and doesn't say much.

↑
Uncle Frank — like Lucy, he's never been married, and I think I know why. He's one of the most booooring people I've ever met. But he's family, so I have to listen to his dull, dull stories.

Looking at that family picture, I can't help noticing that Mom AND both her siblings are single. That can't be a coincidence! One thing's for sure — I'm NOTHING like Mom or Lucy or Frank, so maybe there's hope for me.

The last time we all got together was for Thanksgiving. It was fun to play with Raisa, especially since we hardly ever see her, but mostly it was dull and predictable.

The 5 Things That Happen at Every Family Event

① Uncle Frank will argue with Aunt Lucy about whether fluoride is good for your teeth or a government plot to poison us.

I'm just asking for proof, that's all! Prove to me that fluoride prevents cavities. See, you can't do it! You think it's the fluoride when it's simply the fact that you BRUSH YOUR TEETH! So then why bother with fluoride, eh? Answer me that!

You know, you're a real nut job. Stop drinking tap water if you're so worried about this.

② The main dish — no matter WHAT it is, turkey, meatloaf, brisket, or chicken — will be overcooked and dry.

I don't know what happened this time. I didn't have the oven on too high, I'm sure of that.

Can SOMEONE in this family learn to cook? Every time it's the same thing — a main dish of SAWDUST!

③ Mom will eat too much dessert and moan about it for the rest of the week.

I knew I shouldn't have eaten that second piece of pie! See — now my pants don't fit. This whole family is going on a diet starting TODAY!

④ There will be leftovers for at least a week that will reappear at every meal in different disguises.

First, it's string beans almondine. ↓

Then it becomes string bean frittata. ↓

Then it's transformed into mushed bean casserole. ↓

Mom thinks that putting lots of cheese on something is enough to make it edible, but some things are too far gone for that.

⑤ Cleo will say SOMETHING that makes me want to sink into the floor. (Actually this happens WAY more often than at family gatherings — it's just more embarrassing then.)

That reminds me of the time Amelia's bathing suit came off when she tried the high dive. I warned her that bikinis and diving don't mix, but did she listen? Of course not! It was SO FUNNY!!

Yeah, a real laugh riot.

Okay, it can be painfully boring or embarrassing, but at least I'm used to that kind of family gathering. Now suddenly with my dad I'm part of a HUGE family and in a few weeks I'm going to meet all of them — ALL AT ONCE! They're having an enormous family reunion and, according to Dad, that means Cleo and me now too. What will it be like, facing so many strangers at the same time? It sounds worse than the first day at a new school! I mean, it's one thing to find a place for a dad in my life AND a stepmom AND a half-brother. Now I have to fit in all these other people too? UGH!!

Dad
↓

↑
When I first met him, I thought "Yucch! He looks like Cleo with hairy hands!" But he's like me, too, because we both love to write. He's a reporter for the Chicago Tribune, and when he saw my notebook, he said he'd had one just like it when he was a kid.

George
↓

↑
The first time I saw my baby half-brother, he was about 6 months old. Now he's almost 2 years old and he can walk and talk. He calls me "Mia" because "Amelia" is too hard for him to say, which is better than what he calls Cleo — "Eeoh."

Clara
↓

↑
Dad's second wife (at least I think she's his second one. For all I know he's been married a dozen times). She's a veterinarian, which you would think would make her a super nice person, but you'd be thinking WRONG! She tries way too hard, which just makes her trying.

It's a different family, but I bet there will still be a bunch of predictable things that happen every time they get together. Without knowing anybody, I can guess what some of those things will be. I'm placing bets with Carly on these. If I'm right, she owes me a banana split.

① Somebody will exclaim how great it is that everyone could come. They will use the word "special" at least five times.

② Some kid will get hurt (not badly) and cry ... and cry.

③ Something will be broken. Or spilled. Or both.

④ Somebody's feelings will be hurt.

⑤ Something will be forgotten.

Then there's also my grandparents, great-aunts, great-uncles, and cousins once, twice, and thrice removed. It's way too many people to remember. The worst part is they've all known each other their whole lives. Cleo and I don't know ANYBODY! We hardly know our own dad!

I just had a HORRIBLE thought — the only person there I'll feel comfortable with is CLEO!! That can only be an omen of doom!

That's if I go, of course. Mom says we can stay home if we want.

I understand completely if you don't want to go, and I'm sure your father would too.

It's a lot of strange people to have to face all at once. And I do mean strange.

She doesn't sound terribly fond of Dad's family either.

I didn't want to give Mom the satisfaction of convincing me to stay home, but I wasn't sure I wanted to go. Until Cleo gave me no choice.

Of course I'm going! I had a great time last summer when I visited Dad. I can't wait to meet everyone else.

And I really like Clara. She took me to work with her one day and I got to feed some Great Dane puppies. It was so much fun!

Naturally Cleo and Clara hit it off. Why didn't I notice it before? Their names are almost the same! I'll just call them the Clones (or the Clowns) from now on.

If Cleo's going, obviously I have to go too — even though having her around will make a bad situation way WORSE. Watching her butter up Clara will give me major indigestion. Still, that's better than watching her butter up Dad. And that's better than staying home and letting her become the favorite daughter while I become the far-away, don't-care-about-her daughter.

Anyway, she can be Clara's favorite. I don't care about that. I want to be George's favorite.

He's such an adorable toddler now. I love the way he walks, like his diaper is weighing him down and making him off-balance. When I kiss him on his belly button, he has the best laugh — it makes me smile deep inside.

He even knows some words. Here's some basic George vocabulary:

Baa - his favorite stuffed lamb

La la - his word for light or lamp

Ni-ni - his word for night-night or go to sleep

When I see my dad with George, I think he's a great father. But it makes me sad, too, because he wasn't that kind of father for me. On the plus side, Clara's not that kind of mother for me either. She's just a stepmother (which really means nothing except that she's married to my dad). Mom has her problems, but compared to Clara, she's Mary Poppins.

There are certain things a step-mother should never do. Here's a quick list.

MOTHER

(Yes, a mother can do these things even if you hate it. Come on, she's your mother.)

1. Nag you to clean up your room — you don't have to listen, but she has the right to bug you about it.

2. Make embarrassing suggestions about how to clear up your acne, improve your posture, or select a deodorant.

3. Hug and kiss you in public. I know — it's gross. Just remember, other kids' mothers do it to them!

roll-your-eyes face reserved for Moms only

STEPMOTHER

(No, a stepmother can NEVER do this unless you say it's okay. It's YOUR choice, not hers.)

1. Nag you about your grades, studying, tests, homework, ANYTHING to do with school.

2. Tell you about the facts of life — PLEASE! That's what sex ed. in school is for. It's bad enough coming from a parent, but a stepparent — NEVER!

3. Criticize your hair, clothes, taste in music, anything personal that's none of her business.

So it's all set. Cleo and I will have our first plane trip together with no grown-up around. I hope it's better than sitting next to Cleo on the bus for a field trip — at least then I can open a window to escape her carsick fumes. She'd better <u>not</u> get airsick! If she does, I'm spending the whole flight standing in the back of the plane by the toilets (usually not the best-smelling part of an airplane, but compared to puking Cleo, it'll be a breath of fresh air).

I wrote to Nadia about it. She's the one who encouraged me to find my dad in the first place, so in a way she's responsible for all of this happening — meeting Dad, finding a whole new family, the family reunion, all of it.

Dear Nadia,
  Guess what? Cleo and I are going to a big family reunion in Dallas. It's not for Mom's family. It's for Dad's. So I'll meet all these uncles, aunts, and cousins for the first time. And my grandparents! It's strange to think I suddenly have all these people in my life. Except I'm not sure yet if I really do. Just because you're related to someone doesn't mean you have to care about them. So will they care about me? *yours till the criss crosses, amelia*

Nadia Kurz
61 South St.
Barton, CA
91010

Cleo is totally excited. I'm not so sure. Yeah, I like to see new places and stay in hotels, but not with Cleo. Who can sleep with her snoring? And I'm not crazy about meeting a bunch of strangers. Like I wrote to Nadia, just because they're family doesn't mean I'll like them — or that they'll like me!

This is going to be SO COOL! We'll stay in a hotel and swim in the pool and meet all our family. I'm sure they can't wait to get to know me!

← Sometimes I wish I was like Cleo. She never worries about anything. And NOTHING embarrasses her.

But I'm not Cleo so I can't help feeling nervous. Carly, my best friend, tried to convince me it would be great. I wish she could come with me — then it _would_ be great. Even if no one else talked to me, I'd have her. Now all I have is Cleo, which is like saying all I have is zero or a negative number.

Amelia, you're going to love it. It's always fun to explore a new city, and you've never been to Dallas. And you'll meet some interesting people, I bet.

Carly thinks my dad is great just because he's a reporter and that's what she wants to be when she grows up. So naturally she thinks the rest of his family is also wonderful. I hope she's right — or at least not too wrong.

What if Carly's wrong? What if they're not interesting people? What if they're the most BOOOOOORING people on the planet? Or what if they fight and yell a lot? Or are plain annoying like Cleo, talking with their mouths full and singing off-key? What if I'm trapped in a room full of Cleos?! What a nightmare!

Cleos of all ages, boys and girls, in a horrible sing-along

KUMBAYA KUMBAYA!

Grandma Cleos, Grandpa Cleos, baby Cleos, Uncle Cleos, Aunt Cleos, cousin Cleos

HELP!

I'll never survive.

I <u>had</u> to get that image OUT of my head. So I made flash cards of all the possible types of relatives that are NOT Cleo clones. That way I can be on the alert and know who to avoid (and not think of facing a massive crowd of Cleos).

The Stern, Rigid, Don't-Touch-That Police
Be careful you don't break anything! NO! Don't go near that! Keep your hands to yourself!
The Shove-Food-Into-You-Constantly Feeder
Just try a bite. It's deee-licious! Here, have some. Come on! One bite, just one!
It's so nice to see you, such a special treat!
It's very special that you came. It makes this
a REAL reunion. Really!
Help! You're sucking in all my air!
The Gushy, Too-Close-to-you Talker
The Suspicious All-Kids-Are-Trouble Grump
I know your kind! Swilling soda all the time, eyes glued to the TV, listening to your "music!"
You need some exercise, little missy, some good, hard work!
The Too-Much-Perfume Hugger
GASP!
Now, give us a hug!
I need a gas mask!

I showed Carly my deck of family cards. She laughed but then she said I wasn't being fair — where were all the good types of people? I told her I don't have to worry about __them__. Still, she had a point, so I added a few more cards.

I made up the cousin and aunt stuff because I don't know yet if I have relatives like that. But Carly does, so I know they exist. At least I know George, the cute baby, will be there, so SOMEBODY will be nice to me. And with so many cousins, at least one should be okay.

Finally I added Dad, Clara, Cleo, and me.

The Clueless Dad Who Wants Some Kind of Relationship with You But Isn't Sure What or How Yet

The Annoying Stepmom Who Tries WAY TOO HARD to Be an Instant Best Friend

The Obnoxious Sister Who's an Expert at Saying the Wrong Thing at the Wrong Time

The I'm-Not-Sure-About-All-This-Please-Don't-Force-Anything-On-Me Sister (me)

After all that worrying, it turned out I didn't worry ENOUGH.
Mom took us to the airport and we got on the plane and I was
just beginning to think that MAYBE this would be a fun trip
after all when Cleo took a bunch of papers out of her purse
and started reading them. I wouldn't have paid much
attention, but she was grinning and laughing — way too happy
for ordinary reading. I _had_ to ask her what was so funny.

"Just some e-mails I printed out," she said.

"Why bother to do that? Who are they from?" I asked.

"One of our cousins, Justin. We've been e-mailing and messaging
ever since my last visit to see Dad. Didn't you meet him when
you went? He's SO sweet!"

My stomach sank. No, I hadn't met him. I had no idea who
he was. And now he and Cleo were good buddies and I would be
the ONLY person who didn't know anybody. I didn't say
anything. I didn't want to admit that Dad had done stuff
with Cleo he hadn't done with me (like seeing cousins and
aunts and uncles). But I couldn't lie, either, or
Cleo would find out.

Hmmm, Justin... that
name rings a bell. I think Dad mentioned
him, but his family was out of town when
I was there so we didn't meet. I think
that's what happened.

It may not have been the truth, but it _could_
have been. Why else would Dad not
introduce us?

That's too bad. He's such a great guy. He's in the 8th grade too so we have a lot in common. Plus he's super cute. You know, I guess it doesn't matter that you two haven't met because you're probably too young to be interesting to him anyway.

Cleo has a knack for the cutting remark - OUCH!

I rolled my eyes. Thanks a LOT, Cleo, I thought. Like you're automatically friends with someone just because they're the same age as you. We all know how true that is! As if the whole 8th-grade class are your friends! And as if I'm automatically boring just because I'm in 6th grade. I'm waaaaay more interesting than Cleo, no matter what! I just have to prove that to Justin — and to everyone else.

Ha! Snort! Guffaw!

I hunkered down in my seat and stared out the window. I tried NOT to pay attention to Cleo's snorts and giggles. No way was I going to ask her what was so funny.

This was going to be the longest weekend ever — and not in a good way. I tried to shut Cleo out. I tried not to think about cousins and uncles and aunts. It was enough worrying about a dad, a stepmom, and a part-time brother.

I couldn't help remembering the first time I saw Dad. There was a strange man waiting for me at the airport in Chicago and I knew from his jelly-roll nose that he had to be my dad. I had tried to imagine his face and voice so many times and there he was, right in front of me. He wasn't ANYTHING like I'd imagined. I wanted to run back onto the plane and go home. I wanted to walk right past him and pick out some other, better guy to be my dad. But I didn't. I just stood there until he came over and said, "Hi, you   must be Amelia."

It was SO awkward.

when I →
first saw
him, neither
of us knew
what to say,
we were both
so nervous.

He didn't feel
← like a dad to
me, mostly
because I had
no idea how
that would feel.

→
I couldn't
help noticing
how hairy his
hands were,
but I was polite
and shook his
hand anyway.

And he had that
STUPID teddy
← bear, like he
was expecting
someone else,
not ME.

I'm still not completely comfortable with Dad, but it's a lot easier to be with him now. We're getting used to each other. And now I know that with me first times are usually awkward and tense, not fun and exciting. I just have to remind myself that there's only <u>one</u> first time at a particular thing — after that I've done it before. So no matter how icky this reunion thing is, I might as well get it over with — and the <u>next</u> time I see these people, it'll be <u>much</u> better.

   The flight was pretty short and I didn't have to listen to Cleo guffawing for too long when the plane started to land. As soon as we got off the plane, we saw people with cowboy boots and hats. I guess that's how you know you're in Dallas.

   Dad was waiting for us, along with Clara and George. At least this time there was no teddy bear.

Cleo!

Amelia!

CLEO! You're so beautiful and grown up now! Amelia, nice to see you.

EE-O! MIA!

Dad had a big smile on his face — he sure wasn't nervous <u>this</u> time. First he hugged Cleo. Then he hugged me. Do I always have to come second in EVERYTHING? At least he was happy to see me — that part was good.

Clara was gushing all over Cleo — it was enough to make me queasy. How come she says Cleo's beautiful and not me?

← Even George was happy to see Cleo. I bet if I'd stayed home, no one would have missed me.

Cleo, of course, was beaming.

Dad! Clara! Georgie!

She was supernice and polite, like a totally different person. Now I get it — they think they know and like Cleo, but that's not the real Cleo. It's a pod person, a fake.

The whole way to the hotel, Cleo chattered on and on. I just talked to George. No one talked to me.

Until Dad asked me how I liked Dallas. I said I didn't know yet, all I'd seen was highways and billboards (and the cowboy hats and boots in the airport).

"Well, tomorrow we'll see a real slice of Texas. The family reunion is at an old ranch just outside of town. There'll be hay rides and square dancing and, of course, all the barbeque you can eat."

Yeehaw, I thought. But I didn't say it. If Cleo could be polite, so could I.

"Cool!" Cleo said. "Can I get cowboy boots and a cowboy hat? I want to look like a real Texan!"

I snorted. The only thing she would look like was a real jerk.

But Clara thought it was a great idea. "We should all do that," she said. "Don't you agree, Quentin?"

Dad nodded. "That's the spirit. This is going to be the biggest, best family reunion ever — because you girls are here!"

Cleo smiled. I meant to smile. I tried to smile, but it came out all lopsided. Some things you just can't fake.

Usually I love hotels, but by the time we got to our room I was in a really bad mood. And it just got worse. We weren't staying in a regular room. It was a suite, so Dad and Clara had the bedroom with a crib put in there for George, and Cleo and I were supposed to sleep in the other room on the sofa bed.

IN THE SAME BED!!!!

There aren't enough exclamation marks in the world to convey how awful that ~~thought~~ was.

I said I could sleep on the floor. I said I could sleep in the bathtub. I said I could even sleep in the lobby — ANYWHERE, so long as I didn't have to share a bed with Cleo.

Clara glared at me. "You're both girls. What's the big deal here? I often shared a bed with my sister when we traveled."

That's you, I thought, not _me_. And that's your sister, NOT Cleo. Here's the problem:

HAZARDS OF CLEO

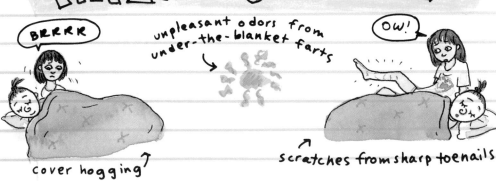

BRRRR

unpleasant odors from under-the-blanket farts

OW!

cover hogging

scratches from sharp toenails

But I couldn't say all that without sounding like a brat. Meanwhile Cleo wore her most angelic face.

It's fine with me to share a bed with Amelia.

I don't mind at all. She can even choose which side she wants.

As if she's the reasonable, nice daughter and I'm NOT!

If I'd known that I'd have to share a bed with Cleo, I DEFINITELY would NOT have come, even if that meant she got to be Dad's favorite. Some things are just not worth it.

But I was already here, so I gritted my teeth and rolled up an extra blanket to go down the center of the fold-out sofa bed. It wasn't the brick wall I wanted, but it was better than nothing.

"Good!" Dad clapped his hands. "I'm glad that's settled. Now we can get our cowboy duds and have some Tex-Mex food for dinner." He used the fake, too-cheery voice he had when we first met. I guess that meant he wasn't comfortable with what was happening.

Good, I thought, glaring at him. I shouldn't be the only one who's miserable. I hope Cleo's snoring is so loud, it keeps him and Clara up all night. That'll show them!

On the way to the car, Cleo and Clara walked together, whispering back and forth. How did they get to be so buddy-buddy? I suppose I should have been glad because that meant Dad had to walk with me, but I got the feeling he was stuck with me more than wanting to be with me.

It's strange, but with Mom, in the Mom-Amelia-Cleo family, I'm the good daughter, the easier one, and Cleo's the one who exasperates Mom and gets on her nerves. In this family, the Dad-Clara-George-Cleo-Amelia one, I'm the problem child. How did that happen?

↓

Who's going to be a big, handsome cowboy? Who is?

Is it Georgie Boy? Is George going to be a cowboy? Yes, he is! He is!

↗
I didn't even try to talk to Dad. My mood was going from bad to worse, from black to blacker.

↑
Dad didn't talk to me either. He just talked to George, another "good" child.

When I was little, I had a mood ring that changed colors according to what I was feeling. At least that's what it was supposed to do. Usually it was dark gray or black, even when I was happy. Now I think it was because I have cold hands, but then I thought the colors really meant something. Anyway, moods are much more complicated than the five choices on the mood ring (sad, happy, jealous, angry, in love). If I invented a ring like that, I'd have a way more complicated scale with LOTS more colors.

Basic Moods

Happy   Sad   Mad   Bored   Scared

Subtle Moods

Tired   Skeptical   Confused   Sneaky   Thrilled

MOOD MEASURE

← On top of the world! Everything's perfect and you're superhappy, like you just won the lottery.

← You're feeling really good, like nothing can go wrong and the future is one long summer vacation.

← You're happy, like you just finished a great book (or, better yet, <u>started</u> one) or ate an ice cream cone.

← You haven't had dessert yet but you know it's coming.

← You just woke up and the day could go either way. Right now it's not good, but it's not bad, either.

← You're a little annoyed, like you stubbed your toe. It's not a big deal — yet!

← You're mad enough to yell and snap but not so mad as to throw things.

← You're furious, out-of-control angry — steam is coming out of your ears.

← You're sad and feel all wilty, like old, limp lettuce.

← You're frustrated, like when no matter how many times you explain something, your mom just doesn't get it.

← You're sad and mad and frustrated all together. You feel like no one loves you and no one ever will. It's the worst feeling EVER!

I would rate Dad's mood a white, George's a purple, Clara's a pink, and Cleo's a yellow. And I'm a definite deep, deep black — all before we've been here 24 hours. That's got to be a record for mood busting.

We drove into an enormous parking lot dominated by a huge neon cowboy hat. On the roof of the building next to it was a life-size plastic cow.

Roy's Cowboy Emporium —
Everything a Dude Needs!

Normally this kind of place would put me in a great mood because it seems like an enormous joke. I mean, a real cowboy store? What would they sell besides hats and boots? Lassos? Chaps and spurs? Saddles? Are there real cowboys anymore? Who buys this stuff — tourists like us, or do people here take cowboys more seriously? I mean, you have to wonder.

Lassos, chaps, spurs, kerchiefs, boots, saddles, belts, bolo ties, hats, suede jackets and vests with fringe at the bottom — you name it, Roy's had it. They even had chewing tobacco and cowboy gum. With all that, I thought I might see a real cowboy in the store shopping for that special something he just had to own. But all I saw were regular people like us who wanted to pretend to be cowboys for a while.

I never knew there were so many kinds of cowboy hats.

↑
brown ones
with leather
strings

↑
black ones
with silver on
the band

↑
white ones
for the good
guys

↑
pink ones
with bows

I picked a
black one
and a blue →
kerchief.

I thought I
looked good. The
funny thing is,
it's hard to feel
bad with a cowboy
hat on. For some
reason just wearing
it made me feel
better. ←

↑
I looked like I was ready for an adventure —
a cattle stampede, a thievin' coyote, or a family reunion!

Cleo didn't settle for just the hat and a kerchief. She went whole hog, making Dad buy her a plaid shirt, suede vest, and bright red boots that clashed with her pink hat. I thought she looked ridiculous, but Clara said she was gorgeous, a real Annie Oakley (whoever that is).

I almost felt sorry for Dad, having to spend so much money, but he could have said no. I think he feels guilty he went so many years without giving us even a birthday present, so now he's trying to make up for it. That's fine

Cleo the cowgirl— or is it just Cleo the cow?

with me. I figure I'll wait until I'm 16 and ask for a car. That's way better than a bunch of goofy cowboy gear.

They even had a hat and boots small enough for George. He looked SO CUTE!

George is another reason it's hard to stay in a bad mood. When he smiles at you, it's impossible not to smile back.

Unfortunately that happy mood didn't last long. It would have been nice to just eat dinner and _not_ talk, but Cleo insisted on asking a zillion questions.

So who's coming tomorrow?

Did I meet them when I was a baby? Do they ask about me? Did they know Mom? Did Mom like them?

Where do they live? What do they do?

I noticed that her table manners hadn't improved, even if the rest of her behavior was fake nicey-nice. I guess it's too hard for her to fake good eating habits.

I have to admit some of her questions were good ones, things I wanted to know too. But mostly I didn't want to think about all the strangers who I was going to meet tomorrow. I didn't want to know whether they liked me or Mom. I could guess the answer about Mom's opinions. I'm pretty sure she hates Dad and everyone he's related to — including Clara and George.

Dad avoided the questions about Mom, but he answered most of the other ones. I wonder what he thinks about Mom. (I sure know her opinion of him!) He never says anything bad about her, but that doesn't mean he doesn't think those kinds of things.

This is a wonderful opportunity for you girls to get to know your family.

I know it's been far too long without them seeing you — now's our chance to catch up. It'll be fun!

Dad likes to focus on the positive.

Clara nodded and chimed in, "It's a lot of people to meet at once. That may make you nervous, but everyone is very nice. I know exactly how you feel because that's what happened to me, too — I met practically the whole family at the same time!"

I glared at her. She had NO idea how I felt — NONE. The last time I visited she invaded my privacy and READ MY NOTEBOOK!! That's a capital offense as far as I'm concerned and proves my point — if she had any sensitivity at all, she would know better. But she didn't. She doesn't. She's absolutely, totally clueless about my feelings.

But Cleo acted like they were soul sisters. I wanted to gag!

You're so right, Clara. Thanks for understanding!

At least I've already met Justin and his family, so they won't all be new faces.

Poor Amelia won't know anyone.

That was it! I snapped!

"Poor Amelia" is just fine! I don't need to know anyone! I don't want to know anyone! I don't know why I bothered to come!

Clara gave me one of her phony, sugary, oh-I'm-so-concerned-about-you smiles. "What can we do to make this easier for you, Amelia? I understand how hard it must be."
"You don't understand anything!" "None of you do! Just leave me alone!" I threw down my napkin and ran to the bathroom.

Luckily it was a fancy bathroom with a sofa in it, the kind that's called a powder room, not a bathroom.

I sat on the sofa and started to cry. The reunion hadn't even begun yet and already everything was going wrong. I wished I hadn't come. I wished I could talk to Carly or Nadia. I wished I had a completely different family, one where there was no divorce.

I stayed there a long time. My eyes were sore from crying and my nose was running. Suddenly I was very tired. All I wanted to do was go to sleep and wake up in my familiar bed in my room at home. Instead I was stuck in a restaurant bathroom in Dallas. What was I going to do?

Someone knocked at the door. I heard Dad's voice. "Amelia, come out. We need to talk."

I didn't want to spend the rest of my life on that sofa, so I got up and opened the door. My knees were stiff and creaky, my cheeks tight with dried tears.

I couldn't look up at Dad or I would start crying again, so I just stood there, staring at his shoes. Now what would happen, I wondered. Would he be mad at me?

Would he send me back to Mom so I wouldn't ruin his big family event? Would he decide that one daughter was enough, he didn't need two? Would he tell me he'd made a terrible mistake answering my letter and he wanted to go back to the way things were before — a great, big silence?

He didn't do or say any of those things. He just hugged me.

It was exactly the right thing to do.

We stood that way for a long time. Neither of us said anything — we didn't need to talk after all. The hug said it better.

Finally Dad pulled himself away and took my hand. "Come on," he said. "It's late. You need to sleep. Tomorrow's a big day."

I nodded. He was right. Tomorrow would be a very big day. I promised myself I'd try to make it a good one. I was here, after all, so I might as well.

That night was the worst night ever. Not because of what happened in the restaurant. Not because of what was going to happen the next day. Because of one big, fat reason —
Cleo!

The sofa bed sagged in the middle, rolling Cleo and me together. No matter how much I tried to sleep on the edge of the bed, I couldn't.

me, staring at the ceiling, wide awake

rolled-up blanket ↓

zzzzzzzz z zzzzzz

Cleo, sound asleep — nothing bothers her!

saggy, saggy mattress

If it weren't for the blanket I'd put between us, we would have been practically on top of each other. As it was, Cleo was way too close to me. I stuck wads of cotton in my ears and I could still hear her snoring. I kept on kicking and pushing at her until finally she rolled over and the snoring stopped. But I couldn't fall asleep. I felt like I was sliding down a cliff — the bed was so caved-in and lumpy. Sleeping on the floor would have been MUCH more comfortable.

I don't remember falling asleep but I must have, because the next thing I knew I had bolted wide-awake, sweating, from a HORRIBLE nightmare.

I dreamed I was in a big corral crowded with people. Everyone was wearing cowboy outfits except me. I was still in my pajamas. I wanted to go home so I could get dressed, but I couldn't find the gate. All I could see were the backs of people with their hats. Everyone was looking at something in the center of the corral.

I squeezed through so I could see what was so interesting. Right in the middle of all those staring, smiling faces was Cleo! She was sitting on a tall stool, playing a guitar and singing.

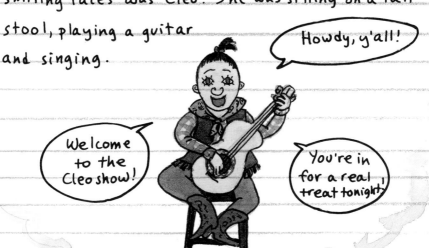

Howdy, y'all!

Welcome to the Cleo show!

You're in for a real treat tonight!

Even though her singing was screechy and off-key, everyone stamped their feet and clapped their hands. They loved her!

I had to get out of there, but a big man who looked like Dad but wasn't Dad — somehow in the dream I knew he was my uncle — grabbed me and shoved me to the front.

"Now, you behave!" he shouted. "Why can't you be more like your sister?"

"I don't want to be like her!" I yelled.

Suddenly everyone turned to look at me, their eyes red with anger and hatred.

"Get her!" someone shouted.

"Don't let her escape!" someone else screamed.

Hands reached for me from all sides. I panicked. I couldn't get away! I tried to yell for help!

And then I woke up.

What a terrible dream! I was afraid to go back to sleep, so I got up and read my book in the bathroom. I seemed to be spending a lot of time in the bathroom these days and I didn't even have diarrhea.

This bathroom didn't have a sofa in it, just a cold tile floor with a small rug on it. This weekend was NOT a relaxing vacation, NOT a fun family visit.   It was turning into the longest nightmare ever.

At breakfast Cleo said she'd slept great. Everyone had. Except me.

I could barely keep my eyes open. →

← I looked like I'd slept under a bed, not on one.

I decided to skip eating and went back to sleep for a couple of hours until Dad woke me up and said it was time to head for the ranch. I had such a bad case of bed head, I was grateful for the cowboy hat — no way I was EVER going to take it off.

I tried not to think about my bad dream and the possibility of it coming true. After all, Cleo doesn't know how to play the guitar. The whole thing was crazy! (Well, she doesn't know how to sing, but she still does.)

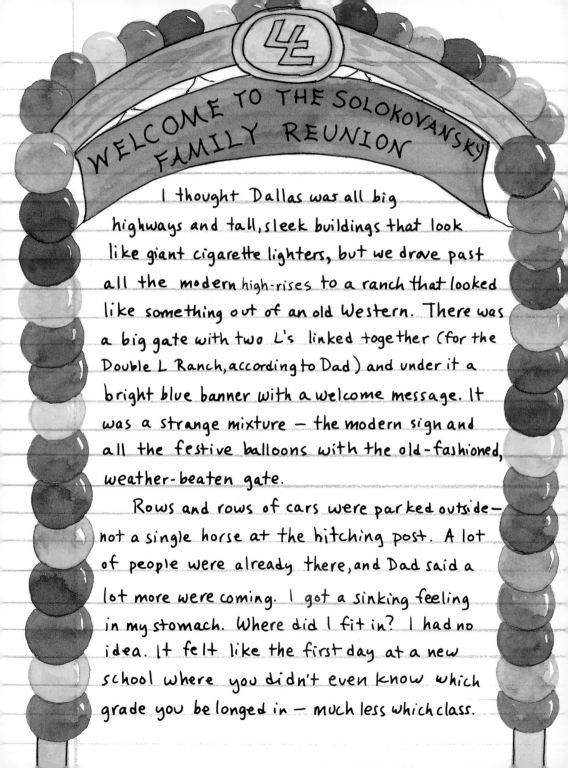

WELCOME TO THE SOLOKOVANSKY FAMILY REUNION

I thought Dallas was all big
highways and tall, sleek buildings that look
like giant cigarette lighters, but we drove past
all the modern high-rises to a ranch that looked
like something out of an old Western. There was
a big gate with two L's linked together (for the
Double L Ranch, according to Dad) and under it a
bright blue banner with a welcome message. It
was a strange mixture — the modern sign and
all the festive balloons with the old-fashioned,
weather-beaten gate.

Rows and rows of cars were parked outside —
not a single horse at the hitching post. A lot
of people were already there, and Dad said a
lot more were coming. I got a sinking feeling
in my stomach. Where did I fit in? I had no
idea. It felt like the first day at a new
school where you didn't even know which
grade you belonged in — much less which class.

I put George in his stroller and felt safer being behind it, like he was a kind of shield. I have to admit, I was impressed by Cleo. She seemed totally fearless. Meeting so many strangers didn't faze her at all.

Either she was incredibly brave or too full of herself to be worried. I wasn't sure which, but either way, I envied her. I wished I could be as calm as her — or like George, completely oblivious to what anyone thinks about him.

The first people we ran into were Dad's parents — my grandparents. How ~~weird~~ ~~wierd~~ ~~weird~~ ~~wierd~~ weird! For most of my life I didn't have any grandparents. Now here they were.

It was even stranger than the spelling of this annoying word!

There you two are! We've been waiting for this moment for so long!

Such grown-up young ladies now!

The last time we saw Amelia, she was little enough to fit inside a shoe box!

My grandmother had Cleo's nose! So that's where it came from! She had bluish hair and bright orange lipstick that made me think of a troll doll. But she wasn't a troll—there was something about her face that was warm and kind.

My grandfather had even less hair on the top of his head than Dad did, but he had these strange long wiry hairs growing out of his eyebrows and ears. He was really old and wrinkled, but his eyes were bright blue and sparkly and young.

I liked them both right away. Maybe deep down my baby self remembered them — we had met before!

Whatever it was, I felt comfortable with them right away. I didn't even mind hugging them. I wanted to call them "Grandma" and "Grandpa," but somehow that was too much. The words stuck in my throat, so I didn't say anything. But I smiled. Maybe this reunion wouldn't be so bad after all.

I wanted to ask a million questions, like did they get along with Mom? Did they try to see us or did they give up like Dad had? Did they visit us a lot before the divorce? Did they approve of Dad marrying Mom in the first place? But I didn't get a chance to ask anything because a big man with a booming voice pushed in front of me to scoop up my grandmother in a bear hug.

I knew he had to be Dad's brother – he had the trademark jelly-roll nose. He looked like the uncle in my nightmare.

I could tell Dad's feelings were hurt — after all, his parents WERE seeing how their grandkids had grown, just different ones than the bellowing man meant.

"Hello, Harold," Dad said. "I'd like to introduce you to my daughters."

Harold turned to us as if just noticing that we existed. He looked at us like he was examining a dent in his brand-new car.

"Chloe? Adelia?" His eyebrows pitched up like they were trying to escape his forehead. "Wow! I forgot you had daughters! What happened? Did that witch of an ex-wife finally let them out of her clutches? Halleluyah, miracles CAN happen!"

I was FURIOUS, but I didn't have to say anything because Dad was even madder than me.

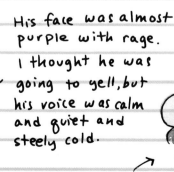

His face was almost purple with rage. I thought he was going to yell, but his voice was calm and quiet and steely cold.

Harold looked totally surprised.

"Harold," Dad hissed through gritted teeth. "I told you the girls were coming. REMEMBER? This is their chance to meet all the family." He put one hand on Cleo's shoulder. "This is Cleo." He said her name **superslowly** and clearly like he was explaining a difficult foreign word. Then he put his other hand on my shoulder. "And this is Amelia. NOT Adelia. And you'll forgive me if I insist that you DON'T insult their mother."

"Oh, hey, sorry," Harold sputtered. "Guess I put my foot in my mouth with that one."

"There's no boot big enough to fill that hole!" Cleo sniped. I was impressed. Go, Cleo, I thought, you tell that jerk! But Dad gripped her shoulder tighter to calm her down.

"Now, now," Harold soothed. "No need to get nasty. We're all family here, aren't we? I said I was sorry, so let's shake and be friends."

Dad nodded. So we did. First Cleo, then me. Yucch! I wanted to wash my hand right away. Then Dad suggested our grandparents take us to get a drink while he and his brother chatted. We didn't need to be asked twice - we were all eager to escape.

I could tell that Cleo was still steamed. It would take a lot of ice to cool her down.

"You have to excuse Harold," Grandma said. (There—I called her Grandma, even if it's only in this notebook.) "He means well. He just doesn't always say the right thing."

"I'll say!" Cleo snapped. "He's a colossal jerk!"

"Come on," Grandpa urged. "He's also your uncle, so you need to see his good side. That's what families do — accept each other, the good _and_ the bad."

Cleo didn't say anything, but she looked at me and I could tell exactly what she was thinking — if this is what it means to have family around then no, thank you! I smiled at her because for once I felt exactly the same as she did.

We found the drinks, passing knots of people on the way who ran up and greeted Grandma and Grandpa or just waved and shouted hello. There were no more introductions and after Cleo and I were settled in a corner sipping sodas, they left us, saying they needed to find our aunts and uncles.

← I put some apple juice in George's sippy cup. The whole drama had passed right by him. Little kids are so lucky!

"This sucks!" Cleo said. "Now they're afraid to talk to us or introduce us to anyone."

"Well, you weren't exactly polite," I pointed out.

"Neither was Harold — and he's a grown-up. He should know better." She slumped back in her chair. "I guess I was expecting everyone to be excited to see us after so long, like we would be the stars of the show. I thought the banner at the gate would say 'Welcome, Cleo and Amelia!' But no one cares that we bothered to come. Harold didn't even remember Dad talking about us!"

Wow. I hadn't imagined anything like that! While I was dreading how horrible this trip would be, Cleo was dreaming of some fantasy, lovey-dovey family reunion. I couldn't help it — I felt bad for her.

She had some kind of Miss America fantasy — like she would be on this big float, blowing kisses at her adoring fans.

The reality had to be a big disappointment. I actually felt sorry for her. That only lasted a minute, though, because some boy came up to us, and Cleo leaped to her feet, grinning, the prom queen once more.

Hey, Justin! How's it going?

Good. I've been looking all over for you. Wanna see the pond out back? It's kinda cool.

Sure, let's go!

Cleo turned to me. "Tell Dad I'm with Justin." Justin looked at me like he'd just noticed my existence.

"Oh, is this your sister?" he asked.

"Yeah, that's Amelia." Cleo was already walking away.

And she'd complained about our grandparents not introducing us to anyone! <u>She</u> was way worse! She could have invited me to join them, but instead they were gone, leaving me alone with George. I should have just said I was coming too, I wanted to see the pond. Now I was abandoned.

I looked at George. "Can this get any worse?" I asked. He didn't have an answer. Neither did I.

I got tired of sitting on the itchy hay bale and decided to take George exploring. →

What else was there to do? I didn't see Dad anywhere. My grandparents were surrounded by loving children and grandchildren. I didn't belong anywhere.

At least George was having a great time. We found the barn with the cows and a pen with sheep and goats. That was enough to thrill him. He was especially excited about the goats. I wished I was as little as him, back to the age when a smelly goat was my idea of fun, and I didn't care if people paid attention to me as long as I was fed and warm.

There were groups of kids running around, playing with each other, but I didn't know anyone and they all looked younger than me. I couldn't just barge in and join them.

I was tempted to go back to the car and wait for the whole thing to be over. I wished I'd brought my notebook with me, but I'd left it at the hotel. Writing and drawing usually made me feel better. Now all I had to distract me was George and he'd fallen asleep. He was still cute, but not much fun that way.

I bumped the stroller over to the far back pastures and watched the horses. There were a couple of young colts, all knobby knees and gangly legs. I couldn't help it—watching them made me smile.

There was one especially small one who was so young, he had trouble organizing his legs.

He kept on wobbling and falling, then unfolding his legs and trying again.

Finally he got it right. He just stood there, looking really tired.

Then a big lump in the grass next to him moved. It was his mother, standing up. I was surprised because you never see horses lying down — they sleep standing up. Then I realized why the colt was having so much trouble with his legs — he must have just been born! That's why the mare had been lying down.

I climbed over the fence and walked slowly over to them. The mare looked at me and snorted, but she let me come close. I could see the foal was still wet from being inside of her. His hooves were soft and spongy and new, not yet hard. I held my breath, touching the colt gently. I felt like I'd been given a gift from the universe, to see someone so soon after they'd entered the world.

Then the mare ambled off and her baby followed. I stood there watching them, full of a strange, calm wonder. It was magical.

"You know how to ride?" The voice startled me. It came from a girl who was sitting on the fence next to George's stroller.

I walked up, shaking my head. "Not horses," I said. "Bikes, yes. I'm not from around here."

"Me neither," the girl said. "We live in Chicago. I'm Tara."

"I'm Amelia and this is my half-brother, George. He lives in Chicago too, with my dad and stepmother. Maybe you know them, Quentin and Clara?"

Tara's face split into a wide smile. "I know George and of course I know your dad and Aunt Clara. I've even met your sister. Cleo, right?"

I didn't know what to say. Everyone knew everyone else — except for me.

"I have a half-brother too," Tara added. "Only he's older, not cute and little. His name is Justin."

Finally! Someone I'd met, if only for a second.

"Oh, I know him! I mean, I just met him today. Is he nice? What's it like having an _older_ half-brother?"

Tara didn't look like Justin and she didn't have a jelly-roll nose → either.

she seemed nice — at least she was someone to talk to. ←

Tara wrinkled her nose. "I guess it's okay. We fight a lot. Dad says that's what brothers and sisters do, but I don't fight as much with my younger sister. I think it's because we have different moms, and Justin only lives with us half of the time, every other week. Plus, he hates my mom, so it's more peaceful when he's gone." She sighed. "At least my mom doesn't have kids from _her_ first marriage. My best friend has 3 half-siblings — one from her mom and two from her dad. It's a mess!"

And I thought _my_ family was complicated! I guess everyone feels that way.

"So my mom is your dad's sister. We see your family a lot since we all live in Chicago. But everyone else here..." Tara shrugged. "Some of them I see only once a year. And some I've never met before. Like you." She stared at me so intently I felt like something was wrong with my face.

Why are you looking at me like that?

Is something the matter?

I was pretty sure I looked okay.

No embarrassing stains or smudges. Maybe she didn't like my hat.

"You're not what I expected, not how Cleo described you," she said. I rolled my eyes. "I bet. That's probably a good thing."

Before we could say anything else, Dad came up.

"There you are! I've been looking everywhere for you." He gave Tara a quick kiss, then told us it was time to eat. I wasn't sure whether I liked Tara or not, but I was definitely hungry and I wanted to eat with <u>someone</u> I knew, not just a bunch of strangers.

Everyone was streaming toward lines of tables that had been set up under awnings. I saw Cleo already sitting next to Justin and stuffing corn bread in her mouth. I noticed she hadn't saved a seat for me.

All I saw were unfamiliar faces until Grandpa waved and caught my eye. Grandma called us over, saying she'd saved us places. Clara looked relieved to see us and jumped up to take George. I realized I hadn't seen her talk to anyone. Maybe she felt as uncomfortable at this reunion as I did.

Dad sat next to Clara and introduced me to his sister, Marta, her husband, Michael, and their daughter, Tina - Tara's sister. Tina stuck her tongue out at me.

Tara nudged me and hissed in my ear. "Okay, I fight with her, too, but you can see why, can't you?"

I nodded, waiting for the lump in my throat to go down, but it was lodged tight. I didn't think I could swallow anything. I felt so alone while Cleo looked completely comfortable, laughing with Justin and shoveling down food.

"Amelia, you're sitting next to me," Grandpa insisted. "We have a <u>lot</u> of catching up to do."

He winked at me and I felt better right away, just with that little wink. →

I know your dad hasn't told you any of the family stories — like how my parents came to America, what life was like before then...

Marta groaned. "Dad, don't bore her first thing. You'll scare her off this family and she'll never want to visit us again."

"No," I said, my voice suddenly unstuck, the lump gone. "I want to hear the stories. Please tell me." I waited. "Please, Grandpa?" There, I'd said it — Grandpa.

He beamed like he'd been waiting to hear those words.

"That's my girl." He turned to Cleo on the other side of the table "How about you, Cleo? You haven't heard the family history either."

"Thanks, Grandpa," Cleo said, the word sliding like butter out of her mouth. Easy for her! Everything was easier for her! "But Justin and I are going on a hayride as soon as we finish lunch. Later, okay?"

I could tell Grandpa was disappointed, but he just nodded. "Go have fun," he said.

Cleo wiped her barbeque-saucy hands and leaped up. Justin followed her. It was enough to make me want to puke, but Marta thought they were "adorable." She said Justin had been looking forward to the reunion for weeks because of Cleo. I wished somebody had felt that way about me. Suddenly Cleo's fantasy of being the star of the show didn't seem so silly — she was certainly the star of Justin's show.

Cleo got an adoring fan and I got family stories. It didn't seem fair.

Cleo, blowing kisses at her doting public. →

SMACK!

SMACK!

Thank you, thank you, everyone! I love you all!

Cleo

Grandpa made a toast, thanking everyone for coming. He named the people who had traveled the farthest and who the new babies were. He didn't mention me and Cleo. I couldn't figure it out — was I part of this family or not?

Then Dad introduced me to his other brother, Jerome, and to his other sister, Julia. At least they got my name right and they didn't say anything mean about Mom. Harold came over too, trying to be all jokey and friendly. I wasn't sure about my other aunts and uncles, but I definitely didn't like him.

No hard feelings, eh, Amelia? I've always liked your mother — she's really something else. You have to understand, divorce is hard on everyone. It's never easy when there are kids involved.

If he said one more cliche, I swear I was going to scream. Lucky for him, he didn't. Instead he invited us over to his house the next day for a big post-reunion brunch. I groaned. That was the last thing I wanted — more reunion after this reunion. I just wanted to go home. I was so relieved when Dad said we had other plans.

"What plans?" I asked after Harold finally walked away.

"NOT going to his house for brunch," Dad said. "ANYTHING but that!" He winked at me.

I laughed. And just that little thing made me love Dad more than ever. I felt like he was on my side and always would be.

The rest of the afternoon there were games like sack races, 3-legged races, bingo, charades, that kind of thing. It was actually fun because I didn't have to talk to anyone. And sometimes it was like being in a big soap opera. After spending several hours with Dad's family I realized there were all kinds of hidden stories and crazy relationships.

FAMILY SECRETS

The wives of Dad's brothers hated each other. ↓

she thinks she's so great!

what a snob!

Clara thought everyone hated her, but they didn't - they just weren't friendly. ↓

why don't they like me?

What have I done?

Harold's kids terrorized Marta's kids — especially Tyler. He was a total bully.

↓

Did Grandpa give you any money? Cough it up! NOW!

Leave us alone!

↑

Tara told me some of these secrets but some I figured out on my own.

Marta, great seeing you again! Putting on some weight there, eh?

And Michael— whoa! Will you look at that gray hair! Must be from dealing with those kids— a real handful, I'm sure.

It's not true that Harold had a good side, like Grandpa said. Either side is yucchy. No one likes him because he's hypercompetitive, always showing off his latest toy (today it was a teeny, tiny digital camera), and he's plain old rude. Why does he say these things except to hurt people's feelings? Why does practically everything he says start with "I" or "my".

Julie's husband, Jeff, is so quiet and shy, no one talks to him. I think he should get together with Clara. Then they'd both feel better.

→

Um, hello... excuse me... um, good-bye...

It all made me realize I wasn't the only one who wasn't sure they belonged. There was no one right way to fit in — it seemed like everyone was finding their own place, even if that place was on the edge of things. Still, there had to be ways to make it easier.

HOW TO SURVIVE FAMILY GET-TOGETHERS
IN 10 EASY STEPS!

① Arrive late — traffic is always a good excuse, no matter what time of day it is, rush hour or not.

So sorry it took us so long to get here.

They were re-paving the road, which meant a total clog. And then that truck lost its load...

② Wear makeup that discourages people from getting too close.

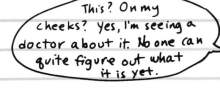

This? On my cheeks? Yes, I'm seeing a doctor about it. No one can quite figure out what it is yet.

Don't worry — I doubt it's contagious.

③ Talk in a thick accent so it's hard for anyone to understand what you're saying.

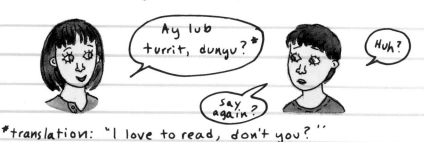

*translation: "I love to read, don't you?"

④ Ask a lot of questions. People love to talk about themselves and that way you don't have to tell them anything about yourself.

Just grunt and nod every now and then.

⑤ Eat — no one expects you to talk with your mouth full.

⑥ Spend time at the drinks table. Mix up experiments, potions, whatever.

⑦ Spend time _under_ the drinks table.

⑧ If you're really bored, go out to the parking lot and try to match the people to their cars.

⑨ Make future plans that you have no intention of keeping.

⑩ Leave early.

Or you can use the Cleo method — escape by spending the whole time with one other person. That method has its own risks, however, if you're not sure how you and the other person will get along for that much time. For Cleo and Justin, that wasn't an issue.

Tara was excited to give everyone the news.

Mom! Guess what I saw!

Come quick— to the barn!

You'll see!

I thought a cat had had a litter of kittens in the hay, something like that, but nooooooo, it wasn't that. It was Cleo and Justin, sitting in the barn, K - I - S - S - I - N - G !

Dad turned purple, Clara was bright pink, Marta was red, and her husband, Michael, was a sickly yellow. Cleo and Justin were surprised. Tara was triumphant.

angry parents

Now you're in for it!

Huh?

Wha..?

Startled teenagers

Smirking half-sister/cousin

The rest of the reunion, all we heard were "kissing cousin" jokes (even though Justin isn't a _real_ cousin). We didn't stay long after that. Dad rushed us all back to the hotel. He was so mad, he didn't know what to say. I felt sorry for him. He's a great dad with George, but he's not used to older kids. Teenagers are beyond him. Especially one like Cleo.

I have to admit, I kind of admired her. She knew how to get what she wanted.

What's the big crime?

She sulked the whole drive back.

That night Dad gave us both a big lecture about cousins and boyfriends and kissing. It was awful — I didn't want to hear any of it and neither did Cleo. We just nodded and said "Yes, uh huh, we understand" until he left. YUCCH!

Once he was gone, I teased Cleo. "I don't think that's what Dad meant by a family reunion."

Cleo stuck out her tongue at me. "Ha, ha, very funny. The worst part is, he'll tell Mom."

I hadn't thought of that. "So?" I shrugged. "What can she do?"

"Never let me out of her sight again!" Cleo huffed. "They both have to leave me alone and let me grow up!"

I got the feeling that what Cleo wanted was a family un-union — at least from Mom and Dad.

I slept on the floor that night on a pile of blankets. It was better than the bed or the bathroom floor.

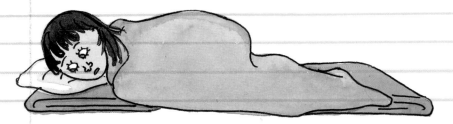

But I couldn't fall asleep. My head was too full of everything that had happened. Now that it was all over, I wondered if it was good I'd come or not.

Should I have stayed home? I was glad I'd met my grandparents. It was good to get a sense of family history from Grandpa's stories. And now Dad's relatives weren't a mystery to me. I still wasn't sure whether I liked some of them or not, but they definitely weren't scary.

All these images flashed through my head.

Chloe?

Adelia?

Uncle Harold, being rude

Grandpa, winking at me

Goat!

You're not what I expected.

George, all excited about the animals

Tara, staring at me

Somehow when you talk to someone while you're in bed, in the dark, everything sounds more secret and important and dramatic. It's a great feeling. →

← You can barely see the other person so their voice takes on a huge presence. It's magical!

"Cleo!" I whispered. "Are you awake?"

"If I wasn't before, I would be now. What do you want?"

"Are you glad you came?" I asked.

"Of course! I got to see Justin, didn't I? I just hope I can go to Chicago again and Mom doesn't ground me for life."

"I guess I'm glad I came too," I said, suddenly feeling sure of it. "And I'm glad I came with you this time."

"You are?" Cleo sounded surprised.

"Yeah." I smiled in the dark. "I like the way you see things sometimes. You're the perpetual optimist while I'm the constant worrier."

We talked for a long time — about families and boys and kissing. And a lot about Dad. Now that I've met ALL his family, he felt more part of mine than ever. I might still be figuring out how I fit in with everyone else, but I KNEW I belonged with him, even if we didn't live together, even if he'd missed practically my whole childhood.

It was the perfect end to the longest, biggest, most-fights-ever family reunion.

I was feeling so good about Cleo, I didn't even mind the flight home with her, but by the next day we were back to normal, fighting with each other like we always do. Mom was happy to have us back home — she was so happy, she didn't seem mad about Justin even. She thought the whole thing was hilarious.

That'll give your father a taste of raising teenagers — teenage gi<u>rls</u>!

I wonder if he'll be so eager to have you visit now!

Like she was sure nothing like that would ever happen while she's in charge. She might be in for as much of a surprise as Dad was.

And I got a postcard from Nadia!

Dear Amelia,
How did the family reunion go? I hope it was a lot of fun. I know how tricky those things can be. At the last one our family had, my aunt walked out in a huff after my uncle insulted her taste in books, and one of my cousins bit another cousin. It was more like going to the zoo than going to a party! luv, Nadia
yours till the sun beams!

Amelia
564 N. Homecrest
Oopa, Oregon
97881

I smiled — that's how families are. But even the worst people have something good about them — like Cleo (though I still couldn't figure out what it was in Uncle Harold's case).

Carly couldn't wait to hear what happened.

She invited me to spend the night so we could talk all we wanted. I couldn't wait to tell her!

I brought her back a   souvenir from Texas— the cowboy hat. She loved it!

We talked until I could see the moon rising outside her bedroom window. I told her about that last night in the hotel with Cleo, how great it was.

"Like it is with us now?" Carly asked. "When we tell each other everything?"

"Yeah," I said. "Just like now."

Neither of us said anything for a while. I was feeling how lucky I was with all my families — Cleo and Mom, Dad, Clara, and George, and here with Carly, my family of friends.

Finally Carly broke the silence. "Good night, Amelia."

"Good night," I whispered back.

And it was.

Amelia's Quick Guide to Surviving Family Reunions

① Smile, smile, SMILE!

② Use the word "special" as much as you can.

③ Don't worry about remembering people's names. They won't remember yours.

Amelia's Itchy ~ Twitchy, Lovey ~ Dovey SUMMER AT CAMP MOSQUITO

by Marissa Moss

(and the camper in Cabin 5, Amelia!)

Simon & Schuster Books for Young Readers

New York   London   Toronto   Sydney

Summer is supposed to be a lazy time, a time to do NOTHING. At least, that's what I think. Mom has other plans. She wants me to go to Camp Runamucka. I told her no way. I told her I'd rather spend the summer in boiling hot Chicago with my dad, stepmom, and half brother. I told her I'd even rather go there with Cleo, the most annoying sister ever, so that shows how much I _don't_ want to go to camp.

Unfortunately, Mom doesn't care what I think.

Don't you realize what a great opportunity this is for you? You're going to have so much FUN!

I never got to go to camp when I was a kid. I hope you know how lucky you are, young lady.

There are three things wrong with what she says.

Wrong Thing #1: Whenever someone tells you how much fun you'll have, you'd better watch out! If you need convincing, if they have to spell it out, how much fun could it be?

mom lost her credibility on that front a long time ago.

It'll be fun to visit Uncle Myron. You can go through his amazing collection of National Geographic magazines!

It's fun going to the dentist — you even get to pick a prize!

why don't you enter that essay contest? It'll be FUN!

The grown-up definition of "fun" isn't fun for kids — it's "you'd better have fun because I'm making you do this whether you like it or not."

Wrong Thing #2: When a parent tells you how tough they had it when they were a kid, it's always a bad sign. It means they expect you to be deeply grateful for some ordinary thing that's no big deal to anyone normal, but it is to the parent.

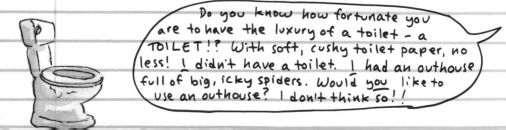

Do you know how fortunate you are to have the luxury of a toilet — a TOILET!? With soft, cushy toilet paper, no less! I didn't have a toilet. I had an outhouse full of big, icky spiders. Would you like to use an outhouse? I don't think so!!

Wrong Thing #3: When a grown-up asks "Do you know how lucky you are?" they don't want an answer. They want you to agree to whatever they say to prove that you're not an ungrateful brat. There's no good answer to this. If you say yes, you've given in to whatever they want you to do. If you say no, they'll force you to do it anyway to teach you not to be such a spoiled, greedy child.

But the MOST wrong thing is that I don't want to go! What if the other girls in my cabin torment me? What if the counselors are ex-prison guards? What if the food is worse than cafeteria food? (Is that possible?) And if I'm gone, I'll miss those things that make summer summer — doing nothing, reading the same comic books over and over again, going to the pool with friends — those are too important to miss. If I don't do them, will I still feel like I've <u>had</u> a summer or will I feel cheated?

WHAT MAKES SUMMER SUMMER

If these things don't happen, have you really had a summer vacation?

① You get an interesting tan line.

Wow! It looks like I'm wearing a T-shirt and shorts even when I'm not!

② You read a really long book you never thought you'd finish.

③ You eat ice cream three times in one day.

④ You invent a new kind of dive at the pool.

⑤ You spend the entire day in your pajamas. Why bother to get dressed?

It's true you can do some of these things at camp — actually most of them. But you can't do the last one and that's the most important one, not having to do ANYTHING at all — even getting dressed.

I was ready to fight Mom on this one. She can't make me have fun. I mean, there's no such thing as Forced Fun. But then she said something that blew away all my arguments.

If my best friend is going, that makes a BIG difference.
Then it really <u>could</u> be fun. Then it's her and me — away
from our families. What could be better than that? I
called Carly right away so we could make plans.

me

Mom said you're going
to Camp Runamucka with me.
It'll be GREAT!

Carly

Yeah! I
read the brochure
and we can ride
horses and canoe and
learn archery and all
kinds of cool stuff!

A summer of no Cleo and lots of Carly — that sounds
terrific! So now I'm excited about camp, but I can't
let Mom know that. I have to slowly, grudgingly give
in. Otherwise she'll think that she really does know
what's fun for me when she still doesn't have a clue.
Even when she's right, I can't agree with her so
quickly or she'll get the wrong idea — the wrong
idea being <u>she</u> knows what's best for me, not <u>me</u>.

I've used this strategy before when Mom wanted me to take guitar lessons and at first I really didn't want to, but then I decided it would be cool to learn to play "Stairway to Heaven." I didn't want Mom to think she could change my mind so easily, so I slowly morphed into agreeing with her.

① First I told her I'd go to a lesson if I didn't have to take out the trash for a month.

I'll be losing a half hour of my precious time for the lesson...

...plus taking time to practice, so I should have some way to get back my lost free time.

No trash chore for a month buys back a little of that time. Is it a deal?

That worked great because I seemed reluctant about the lessons PLUS I got out of trash duty.

② Then I pretended going to guitar was like going to the doctor's for a shot. On the ride to and from the lesson, I said hardly anything.

me, scowling and slouching →

what are you playing now?

← Mom would act all nice and chatty while I glared out the window in as LOUD a silence as I could make. But I wouldn't argue or yell. That part was over.

③ Then eventually I acted like it was totally normal to go to guitar. Mom couldn't stop smiling.

I'm SO glad you're getting something out of these lessons. It's a good thing I made you do it — think how proud you'll be when you can play!

yeah.

The key is NOT to be enthusiastic about it — keep your tone neutral.

I'll do something like that for summer camp — a gradual softening of attitude so Mom thinks she's convinced me of something. I used to be more stubborn about these things. If I started out disagreeing with Mom, I could NEVER admit she was right even when I figured out later that she was. Now I'm better about that, but I still need a slow change, not a quick shift, or I feel like I'm giving in too much.

There's a way to grade this kind of stubborness. I call it the Measure of Muleness. I used to fall in the Hard as Rock category, but now I'm much better.

Hmmph! I call stubborn mules "teenagers." You know the expression — "stubborn as a teenager!"

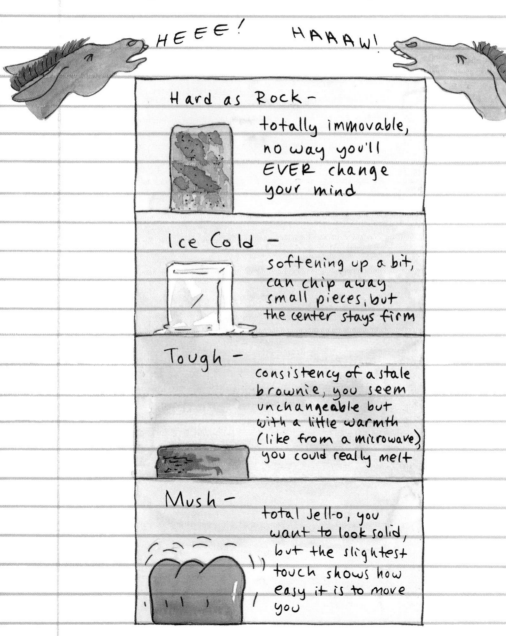

I'm about at the stale brownie stage now, almost chewable. I told Mom as long as she gives me lots of Bug-Off to pack, I'll go to camp. And maybe I need a snakebite kit and some mousetraps too.

Carly made a great list of absolutely essential equipment we _have_ to bring to camp. Unfortunately, her list and Mom's are total opposites — except they both include clothes and flip-flops.

← Carly's To-Pack List　　　　Mom's To-Pack List ↘

Carly's To-Pack List	Mom's To-Pack List
nail polish (3 different colors for a change of pace)	underwear
books and magazines	socks
flip flops	shorts
sketchbook or notebook	T-shirts
pens and pencils	sweatshirt
tiny flashlight	jeans
candy	toothpaste, floss, toothbrush
junk food	shampoo, soap
clothes	pj's
bathroom stuff	bathing suit
binoculars	sunblock
telescope	bug spray
bikini	flip-flops
big beach towel	hairbrush
sunglasses	stamps for letters home
lip gloss	

This ALL sounds good!

There's NOTHING fun about this list!

Any list that starts with underwear CAN'T be good!

I just combined the two lists and Mom actually said yes to everything — except the telescope and binoculars because she's afraid they'll get stolen or broken. I was really beginning to get excited about camp.

Then Mom said:

I'm glad you're changing your attitude about camp.

It will be a great experience for you and Cleo.

CLEO!!!

I panicked! Going to the same school as Cleo was bad enough, but going to the same camp! That was unsurvivable! First I was upset. Then I was furious.

steam

You said I'd be going with CARLY!

NOT Cleo! You tricked me!

I couldn't help but think of the time Cleo went on the science field trip with my class — it was MY MOST EMBARRASSING MOMENT EVER!

Cleo didn't see what the problem was. She thought it was fine for us to go together. →

I'm taking the counselor-in-training course so I can work at summer camps. I'm not really in camp at all.

What's the big deal? I'll be with the older kids — far away from the little kids like you.

I bet we'll never even see each other.

Mom said Cleo was right and I should stop acting like a baby. I was still mad, but when I told Carly about it, she said the same thing. She tried to convince me we'd still have fun.

"Who cares about Cleo?" she said. "She won't be in our cabin or our group. We won't even eat meals at the same time, I bet. It'll be like she's on another planet."

I wanted to believe her. "I guess you're right," I said. Really, I hoped she was right, but I had a sinking feeling she was wrong, wrong, wrong.

I have to give Cleo some credit, though. When it was time to take the bus to camp, she didn't even try to sit next to me. She sat in the back with some other kids she knew. I sat next to Carly and I could almost pretend Cleo wasn't on the bus at all — just me and my best friend, going away together.

Which would have been great except we were going away in the smelliest, grossest way possible — on the camp bus. We tried to find a good seat, meaning one that _wasn't_ sticky, didn't have gum on the back of it, and was next to a window that actually opened.

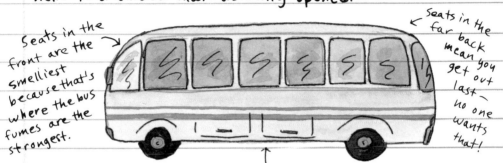

Seats in the front are the smelliest because that's where the bus fumes are the strongest.

← Seats in the far back mean you get out last — no one wants that!

Seats in the middle are the bumpiest — you practically hit your head on the ceiling every time the bus hits a pothole.

We ended up somewhere between the middle and the front, but nothing could save us from the singing that filled the whole bus. For some reason, teachers and camp counselors think that singing stupid songs makes a long drive seem shorter. Really it's the other way around — you can't believe you'll have to listen to _another_ chorus of 99 Bottles of Beer on the Wall and yet you do. There's always time for another round.

...you take one down and pass it around...

By the time the bus pulled into camp, Carly and I were ready to jump out the window.

We needed fresh air! We needed to get off our sore rear ends and we needed a break from off-key singing!

After the torment of the bus ride, the camp looks great. It isn't smelly, crowded, or noisy. And there are no mean kids in my cabin — at least that I can tell. One girl, Kayla, is too busy crying from homesickness to have the energy to be mean. She hasn't been gone for even one whole day and already she misses everyone and everything at home really, really badly. If she's this sad now, what will she be like after a week?

The other girls try to make Kayla feel better, and our counselors are being extra, extra sweet to her.

↑
Paris — she's a master of long, involved jokes that are HILARIOUS!

↑
Miri — she's on the swim team back home and plans to spend as much time in the water as possible.

Kayla →

I feel bad for her, but I wonder what's at home that's good enough to cry _this_ many tears over.

↑
Yuki — she's very shy. She's barely said two words yet — and she didn't sing on the bus.

Each cabin has two counselors. Ours are Crystal and Jolene. Crystal isn't a real name, it's a "spirit" name, whatever that means.

← Crystal aka Lorraine

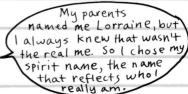

My parents named me Lorraine, but I always knew that wasn't the real me. So I chose my spirit name, the name that reflects who I really am.

↑ she's
Layla — crazy about horses and wears riding boots all the time.

Crystal is also big on aromatherapy and astrology. She took roll by trying to guess our astrological signs. She thought I was a Libra and that Carly was a Cancer. But I'm a Pisces and Carly is a Libra, so she was totally mixed-up. She still thought <u>we</u> were wrong, not her.

Julia — she's like a mother hen, always trying to make sure everyone's okay.

You're _sure_ you're not a Libra? Maybe you're on the cusp or your moon is in that house. You have a <u>lot</u> of Libra energy.

← I thought she was going to SMELL me to see what my aroma revealed about me.

↑ Crystal

Bianca — she's a master of tricks. She promises she'll teach us how to short sheet a bed.

Jolene is the complete opposite. She's studying to be an engineer, so she knows a lot of stuff about science and machines. She and Crystal tease each other that Jolene can teach us useful things like knot-tying, starting a fire, using a compass, and Crystal can show us the constellations and how to make scented candles and tie-dye shirts. They're a good combination.

Paige — she's a little home-sick, but Bianca's her best friend, so she's okay.

Amrita ↑ — she's bossy, but Jolene's great at handling her and keeping her from controlling everything.

I'm not going to show you what the stars tell you about your personality, but I will teach you how to use them for navigation. Who knows where the Polestar is?

↑
Jolene

Yumi ↑ — she's a HUGE Harry Potter fan and brought all the books to reread at camp!

I'm beginning to think camp will be fun after all, even if Cleo is here — somewhere. The counselor-in-training group is pretty separate. They even eat at different times, so I haven't seen Cleo since we got off the bus. Sometimes I think I hear her distinctive guffaw-laugh, but when I turn to look, it's never her, just some other kid with a laugh like Cleo's. (Poor kid!) Carly keeps telling me to forget about my sister. I'm trying, really I am.

Carly is already deep into the camp experience. → She says she has 3 goals for the end of our time here.

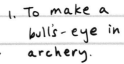

1. To make a bull's-eye in archery.
2. To swim all the way across the lake.
3. To be named editor of the camp newspaper.

Carly impresses me because she knows herself really well. I mean, she knows what she wants, what she's good at, and what she needs to work on to get where she wants to be. Sometimes those things aren't so clear for me — like I think I want something, but when I get it, it turns out I didn't _really_ want it after all. Or I think I'm good at something when I'm not, I'm just average. Or I think I'm a complete failure at something when I'm actually pretty good, I just have to try hard to succeed.

I'd like the same 3 goals as Carly except I don't want to be newspaper editor. Instead I'd like to be a staff cartoonist. And I'd <u>like</u> to make a bull's-eye, but I admit that's probably not going to happen, so I need a more reachable goal — like hitting the target at all.

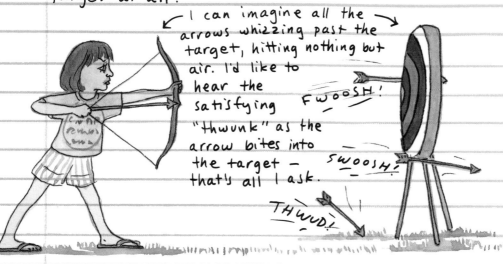

I can imagine all the arrows whizzing past the target, hitting nothing but air. I'd like to hear the satisfying "thwunk" as the arrow bites into the target — that's all I ask.

FWOOSH!

SWOOSH!

THWUD!

Our first night we stayed up late singing around the campfire (not at all annoying the way bus-singing is). It wasn't just our cabin, but all ten cabins in our group. That's a lot of kids, so it was a BIG campfire! I loved smelling the smoke, watching the flames crackle and pop, and picking out the constellations in the black, black sky — way darker than the sky ever gets at home. I would never admit it to Mom, but it was FUN.

There were so many stars, it was like a giant dot-to-dot in the sky. I found all kinds of amazing, new constellations.

The Giant Jelly-Roll Nose — watch out! It's gonna blow!

The Heavenly Marshmallow, get ready to toast!

The Flying Canoe — now I just need to find the Celestial Paddle.

The Big Mosquito — quick, get the Bug-Off!

The Starry Poison Oak — whatever you do, DON'T TOUCH IT! →

me ↘

Carly ↙

I didn't sleep too badly considering the noise of several people snoring, the occasional whispers and farts (PU!), and the paper-thin mattress I slept on. I could face the chilly bathroom with all the big spiders in the corners. I could handle washing my face with cold water and listening to eleven other girls brush their teeth, but breakfast was something else! Talk about bad manners — chewing with open mouths, slurping, and burping. It was like having Cleo at the table ALL AROUND ME!

And then there was the food itself.

There's a scale of awful institutional food, from airplane meals to school cafeterias to camp food. Camp food is some of the best AND some of the worst.

BAD   CAMP   FOOD

soggy, canned green beans — never good ANYWHERE!

barfy baked beans

lumpy oatmeal

watery hot chocolate

slimy lima beans

No bean is a good bean unless it's a jelly bean!

hobo stew — another name for leftover mush

stale, hard rolls — nothing is fresh EVER!

canned pineapple as if it's a treat

The good camp food all has one essential ingredient that makes it taste great — a campfire. Anything cooked in, on, or over a campfire is DELICIOUS, especially if you eat it outside under a starry sky.

GOOD CAMP FOOD

banana boat
(dive in!)
↓

pocket stew
↓

↑ Peel back one strip from the banana peel, slice off the top of the banana, put chocolate chips and mini marshmallows where you sliced, fold the peel back down, wrap in foil, and bake in the coals for ten minutes — yum!

↑ Fill a piece of foil with chunks of potato, carrots, and peas, fold into a pouch, and set on a forked stick. Cook over the fire for half an hour, then munch!

↑ walking soda — take an orange and roll it on a hard surface until it's all mushy. Take a peppermint stick, bite off both ends, then poke it into the orange. Use the peppermint stick as a straw to suck up the juice.

Pocket peach pie ↑ — sprinkle cinnamon and sugar on a peeled peach. Wrap in foil and bake in coals for twenty minutes — ta da! Dessert!

And of course, there's always s'mores!
↓

↑ Add peanut butter   or caramel sauce ↖

↑ or make the classic version — the essential camp food! Have s'more!

Kayla seems a little better today, not quite so homesick, or maybe she's too exhausted to miss anyone now because we went on a loooooooong hike. I feel like my blisters have blisters! Our reward for so much exercise was to get the afternoon free for whatever we wanted. Most kids went right to the lake. That's what I wanted to do too, but Carly had other plans. She wanted to sign up right away to work on the camp newspaper, quick, before all the jobs were taken. I said there was no rush, it's summer, who wants to do extra work, but when Carly gets an idea like that, there's no talking her out of it.

I dreamed of floating on a raft. Carly dreamed of being an ace reporter.

↓

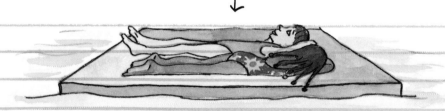

She's my best friend, so even though the cool, crystal clear water was calling to me, I went with her to the cafeteria where all the newspaper wanna-bes were meeting.

I thought there would be just a couple of kids, but there was almost a dozen, plus one camp counselor, Jeff, who's in charge of the newspaper.

Jeff had a long ponytail, a moustache, and a goatee, as if he couldn't get enough hair — he needed more, wherever he could grow it.

I think of reporters as high energy, aggressive-type people, but Jeff was calm and soft-spoken. There was nothing urgent about him at all. I couldn't imagine him yelling, "Stop the presses! This is page one stuff!" Or even "Extra, extra, read all about it!"

It's good to see so many of you turn out for this meeting. Together we can put out a great little newspaper — and have fun while we're doing it.

After a short introduction about the newspaper (how many pages, how often it comes out, what it covers), * Jeff divided up the jobs that needed doing. Then he passed around a piece of paper and asked us to sign up for our first three preferences.

*answers: 2 pages, once a week, camp news

Carly wanted to list hers as 1) editor, 2) editor, and 3) editor, but she knew that wasn't what Jeff meant by three choices. So she wrote down 1) editor, 2) columnist, and 3) reporter.

"What's the difference between a reporter and a columnist?" I asked. I should know this since my dad works for a newspaper, but I don't even know which one he is or what he does exactly.

"A columnist writes short essays about their opinions, like I could do a column on what makes a good name for a camp and what doesn't. A reporter writes about things that happen — newsworthy things, like who won the s'more-eating contest or how a skunk sprayed Cabin 6." Carly really knows her stuff.

You should interview me for my side of the story.

There could be a feature → article about how to make the best s'mores next to the story about the s'more-eating contest. The same reporter could write both. Then the columnist could write about her personal search for the ideal s'more. It would be an all-smore issue!

caramel ↓

peanut butter ↓

whipped cream ↓

Add caramel or peanut butter or whipped cream — or all three — for more of a s'more!

I like the idea of being a reporter or a columnist, but my first choice is to be a cartoonist. I'd love to do a weekly strip. I know it can be a lot of pressure coming up with funny things to write about every week, but for the six weeks of camp, it's not that much, only six comics. I can do that. So I put down my choices as 1) cartoonist, 2) columnist, 3) reporter. I wondered what the other kids chose.

There was a group of boys who were good friends. ↙

There was a boy who doodled the whole meeting. ↙

I bet he put down cartoonist as his first choice too.

There was a girl who was very bossy. (I'm SO glad she's not in our cabin!) She interrupted Jeff constantly, talking about what she did last year in journalism class. I can tell she wants to be editor and tell everyone else what to do. ↑

↗ whatever they do, they'll want to do it together, so I'm guessing they'll be reporters or maybe work on page layout as a team.

Listento me!

Jeff said we'd know our positions by the end of the day. He's going to post them by the cafeteria door. Then the meeting was over.

And there was a girl who thought she was Ms. Star Reporter. The less said about her, the better!

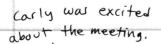
Carly was excited about the meeting.
↓

I was excited that it was over so soon.
↙

This is going to be great — our own little newspaper! All ours.

Yes, and the best part is we can still go to the lake. C'mon, let's go swimming!

Okay, okay. I got my dose of journalism for the day, you can get your relaxation time.

After all, it IS summer, remember? Journalism is WORK!

The lake was as wonderful as I thought it would be. The water was so clear, you could see the bottom. I don't like swimming in dark water — that's kind of creepy.

I can't help imagining some giant fish is going to bite me when the water's too black to see in. Or if there isn't a fish, there'll be an evil eel which is even worse!

But this water was perfect — not too hot, not too cold, crisp and clear. There was a raft floating in the middle of the lake that was the perfect place to relax in the sun.

Carly and I stretched out and watched → the other swimmers.

It was a wonderful, lazy summer day, almost like not being in camp at all. ↑

"There's that boy who was at the newspaper meeting." Carly pointed to a kid diving from a rock.

"He's a good diver," I said. "I bet he ends up being a cartoonist for the paper."

"Why do you say that?" Carly asked.

"He was drawing the whole meeting. Kind of like me."

Carly gave me a look — a strange look, one I'd never seen on her face before and I couldn't tell what it meant. She seemed annoyed at me but I hadn't done anything, said anything, to bug her. I didn't get it.

"Is something the matter?" I asked.

"No! Why should something be the matter?" That's what she said, but her tone said yes, something's bugging me. "I'll race you back to the shore," she challenged. She didn't wait for an answer — she dived right in.

Talk about changing the subject! I jumped in after her and swam as fast as I could, but she still beat me.

I forgot about the boy until dinner when I saw the list Jeff had posted with the newspaper jobs. Carly didn't get to be editor-in-chief, but she is a columnist. I got my first choice — cartoonist. And so did the boy, just like I guessed. Now I know his name — it's Luke.

we all checked the list at the same time.

I told Carly she should be happy — she's the only columnist. There are several reporters, one photographer, a couple of layout, design people, one editor, and two cartoonists. For such a small newspaper, it's a pretty big staff.

But Carly wasn't happy.
↓

It should be MY staff. I should be in charge.

I bet Jeff picked Mike because he's a boy — that's so sexist!

I thought maybe Carly was right — she didn't get the job because she's a girl. But the next day we had another meeting and I could see why Mike was made editor. He has a <u>lot</u> of journalism experience. Plus he's a nice guy, not the kind of person you can stay mad at. And he's cute — that makes it even harder to hold a grudge.

Even Carly had to admit that he was a good choice.
↓

↑
The star reporter girl was upset that she's not the ONLY reporter. She wanted at least the title "Lead Reporter." All she gets is "reporter." I wish she'd stop whining about how she was cheated!

Okay, people, we have a lot of work to do and not much time. Let's put out a paper!

We went on a really long hike today and Carly talked about ideas for her column the whole time. I love Carly. She's my best friend, but by the end of the afternoon I wasn't sure which was more exhausting — walking or listening to her.

My feet were so sore, it felt like my blisters had blisters.

My ears were even more sore. They were red and achy from the weight of so many words.

blah, blah, blah

blah, blah, blah, blah

I felt like the words were leaking out of my ears, there were so many of them crammed in there.

But Carly wasn't at all tired. She was still talking.

Maybe I should write an article on surviving long hikes, what to bring, that kind of thing...

...or I could write about my views on arts and crafts, which are the most crafty...

...or I could do a collection of camp songs — that'd be fun...

ENOUGH ALREADY!

Write about ANYTHING!

Write about EVERYTHING!

Just DON'T talk about it first!

"Well," Carly said, "aren't you grumpy! I was only trying to have a conversation about my column. I thought you'd want to talk about it since you're my friend."

"Yes, I'm your friend." I was exasperated. "But that wasn't a conversation. It was a long monologue you were having with yourself. I just happened to be nearby."

Carly laughed. It's a good thing she has a sense of humor or she'd be furious with me.

"You're right," she admitted. "I was really thinking out loud. It's just that I'm excited to have a column. I really want it to be great."

"And it will be," I said. "Now I need to work on my cartoon. I have to come up with some ideas too, you know. And mine have to be funny."

So while Carly worked on her column, I got started on my comic strip. I didn't even know who I wanted my characters to be. I had a <u>lot</u> of work to do.

possible comic strips
↙

I know, I know — it's BAAAAAD!

Why are all my characters food? Why are all my stories about being eaten? Maybe I need a snack.

Those were terrible. I needed a theme, like camp letters home or campfire stories or camp gossip. I decided to go for a walk to get some inspiration — a walk around camp, not a hike.

I found Luke down by the lake, sketching his own comic. I asked him if I could see, and he said sure.

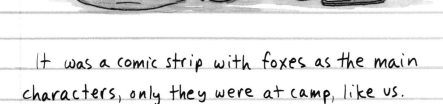

It was a comic strip with foxes as the main characters, only they were at camp, like us.

WHAT ARE YOU MAKING YOUR LANYARD FOR?

YOU DON'T MAKE LANYARDS FOR ANYTHING, THEY'RE A ZEN ACTIVITY, A FORM OF MEDITATION.

WHAT ARE YOU MAKING A LANYARD FOR?

IT'S A ZEN THING, A MEDITATION. OH, FORGET IT— IT'S FOR MY BACKPACK.

COOL.

It was really good. I told Luke how much I liked it, and how I hadn't even started mine yet. We talked about how hard it is to get ideas and make them come out the way you want them to. We talked about comic book artists we like and don't like and why. We talked for so long, the dinner gong rang and I still hadn't done my comic. It was so easy to talk to Luke, I almost forgot he was a cute boy. He was something even better now — a friend.

We walked back to the cafeteria together and it all felt so normal and comfortable.

↓

↑

Until Carly saw us.

Then it suddenly felt strained and awkward and totally uncomfortable.

Carly almost looked like she was mad, but trying hard not to look it. →

There you are! I've been looking for you, Amelia. I thought you were working on your comic.

I guess not.

"I _was_ working on it," I explained. "Then I ran into Luke. He's already finished his comic – it's great."

Luke smiled. "I hope Mike thinks so."

Carly flashed a big smile. Suddenly she was super friendly, only not to me, to Luke.

"Oh, I'm sure Mike will," she cooed. "I think he's a good editor, don't you? He _really_ helped give me direction for my column. I'm writing a column, you know."

"Yeah," Luke nodded. "How's it going?"

Carly's smile grew even bigger. "How sweet of you to ask! Want to eat dinner with me and I can tell you about it?"

"Sure," Luke said, and they both headed for the line to pick up a tray.

I followed behind, acting like I was part of their

group, only I wasn't. Carly shut me out — my best friend!

They chatted all through the line as they picked up enchiladas, beans, and rice. Neither of them said anything to me — not one word. Then Carly led the way to a table that conveniently only had two seats left.

"Oh, sorry, Amelia." She turned to me. "I guess you'll have to find another table."

"Yeah," I said slowly. "I guess I do." I sat next to Kayla, feeling like steam was coming out of my ears.

I was so mad, I bit into my food like it was an enemy.

I chewed furiously. I didn't know you could chew angrily, but you can. Nothing tastes good, but it's satisfying to gnash and mash.

"What's wrong?" Kayla asked. "Are you homesick too?" She sniffled. "I talked to my mom today and I feel much better."

"Good for you," I snapped.

"Well, you don't have to be mean about it," said Kayla. "I'm just trying to be friendly."

"You're right — I'm sorry." I felt bad. It wasn't her fault that Carly was being so mean. "I had a fight with my best friend, so I'm not exactly in a friendly mood."

"Oh," said Kayla. There was a long pause. "Well, at least you're not homesick."

But I was homesick, homesick for Carly. I watched her laughing and talking with Luke and I missed her. She should have been doing that with <u>me</u>. I liked Luke, but I didn't like him taking Carly away. And I didn't like Carly taking Luke away — after all, <u>I</u> was talking to him first.

The more I watched them, the more jealous I got. Only I wasn't sure who I was jealous of — Luke or Carly.

I wanted both of them to be my friends, not each other's.

They looked so happy together, it made me feel worse.

When I left the cafeteria, they were still talking. I went back to the cabin and tried to work on my comic. I didn't get anything made except for a big pile of crumpled-up papers, all comic rejects.

↓

I had already washed up and brushed my teeth by the time Carly got back. I was in a black, black mood, and she looked so happy she was practically floating.

"Isn't Luke perfect?" she burst in. "He's so sweet and smart and funny. And cute, so cute!"

"Yeah," I said, "adorable. So adorable you dropped me. That's a horrible way to treat a friend. You like a boy, so suddenly I'm invisible?"

"I did that?" Carly looked startled, then guilty. "I guess I did. Oh, Amelia, I'm sorry. It's just that I really, really like him."

I wasn't letting her off the hook yet. "Yeah, I can see that. Everyone can see that. But does that mean you can treat me so badly, like you barely know me?"

"You're right, Amelia, and I said I was sorry." Carly sounded grouchy. Maybe I'd pushed too hard, but a simple "I'm sorry" didn't feel like enough. I'd come all this way to this stupid camp to be with my best friend, not to have her dump me so she could be with a boy, especially a boy who was MY friend first.

   We went to bed mad at each other. It felt terrible. I couldn't fall asleep for a long time and when I did, I had a nightmare.

   Carly and Luke were whispering to each other and walking like they were glued together.
   They walked right by me.
   I said hi, but they ignored me. I felt invisible.

Then it got worse — they started kissing in front of me like I wasn't there. "Stop it!" I yelled. "Stop it NOW!"

But it didn't matter how loud I screamed. They kept on kissing and my throat got redder and sorer. I wanted to shove them apart, but I couldn't move. It was that horrible dream sensation of your feet being stuck in mud and there's no way to free them.

Finally, I was so exhausted, I collapsed on the ground and started to cry. There were no more screams left inside of me, just tears.

Then I woke up and I was really crying. My pillow was wet from tears.

I felt stupid crying in my sleep.

And I felt sad — very, very sad.

I can't lose Carly, I told myself. I'm not going to let a boy ruin our friendship. She can have Luke as a boyfriend — I don't care about that — but she has to keep me as a best friend, no matter what.

Once I decided that, I could go back to sleep and this time, I didn't dream anything. When I woke up, the first thing I did was talk to Carly.

I'm sorry I was mad at you yesterday. It's just that you're really important to me. I don't want a boy to come between us.

I don't want that either. We're too good of friends for that. But c'mon, Amelia, you can't be jealous of a boyfriend — if that's what Luke becomes. We have to agree that it's okay for each of us to have boyfriends, so long as we don't let them get in the way of _our_ friendship.

I agree! That's exactly what I want— our friendship comes first.

It was a beautiful, sunny morning, even sunnier because Carly and I were friends again. Breakfast is normally the worst meal at camp (no campfire, no starry skies), but even that was great today. Carly didn't even glance around to find Luke in the dining hall (like I did). We ate together as if we'd never fought.

The squirrels begging for food by the windows gave us each a good idea of what to do for the newspaper. Squirrels are furry and cute, but the counselors say we should NEVER feed them. They're not pets, they say, they're wild animals.

So that's what Carly and I are going to do, each in our own way — Pet Peeves and Pet Loves. Carly is going to interview kids and do a column on what people like and hate about camp, a kind of quick top ten list of each.

I'm doing the same thing, only as a comic strip and it's my own list, not other people's. We're going to ask Mike about having both things next to each other on the page.

I love it that Carly and I are more than just friends — that we can work together like this and inspire each other. We give each other our best ideas.

The finished version was smaller and neater, so it looked more like a comic.

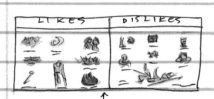

Except there weren't many speech bubbles, so it was a ← free-form kind of thing.

Carly said it looked like a page out of my notebook. I guess that's the easiest way for me to think and draw.

Carly's column was really funny. I thought our pieces worked great together.

See! That shows what great friends we are. We belong together. We can't fight over a boy — that's ridiculous.

You're right. There's no reason to fight at all. I'm sorry everything got blown out of proportion. I mean, liking Luke doesn't mean I like you less.

Of course not! You're my best friend, no matter what!

No matter what!

I really believed that. I didn't see any reason Carly couldn't have her little crush on Luke and still treat me like her best friend.

Then we had the newspaper party.

It wasn't really a party — it was a dinner where we all worked putting the paper together. We ate pizza, did final edits, played around with page layouts, then printed out the finished newspaper. It was a LOT of work and by the time it was over, we were all silly from being so tired.

Luke and I worked together on scanning and resizing our comics. We talked about our favorite comic websites and who the most interesting writers and artists are. The more we talked, the more I noticed how cute he was, how sweet and smart and sensitive. I was beginning to wish he was more than a friend. I mean, I really liked him — "like" like, not just like. And I wondered, did he like me?

The bossy girl who didn't get to be editor wasn't bad after all. She worked HARD!

way more than Ms. Star Reporter who just whined.

She said her talents were being wasted. What talent, I wondered.

I couldn't help it — I found myself staring at him. →

Then I thought, is this what Carly feels? She can't like him this way. I want him to like me, not her.

Carly was busy with Mike most of the time but every now and then, I saw her looking in our direction and she didn't look happy. Once she even shook her finger at me and mouthed "What are you doing?" At least, I think that's what she was saying — that or "Cock-a-doodle-doo." I just shrugged my shoulders.

When she was finished, Carly came over to us, only she wasn't the Carly I knew at all. She was all fake smiles, tilting her head to the side, even her voice was different, all sugary and soft.

Jeff went from kid to kid, encouraging everyone to do their best work. Maybe <u>that's</u> what turned Carly into a major flirt. She was working it, alright!

I love your comic, Luke! It's the best part of the whole newspaper!

I swear, she was practically batting her eyelashes! I thought that only happened in cartoons.

That's sweet of you to say, but I think Amelia's comic is way better than mine. I laughed out loud when I read it!

I wanted to jump up and hug him! Not only was Luke NOT falling for Carly's nicey-niceness, he said good things about me — ME! That proved he liked me __better__. I glared at Carly. "See!" my eyes said. She glared back. "Oh, yeah?!" her eyes replied.

We gave each other the evil eye while trying to seem normal and friendly, so Luke wouldn't suspect anything. It wasn't easy. In fact, it was awful, but I couldn't leave because I wanted to be with Luke — and that was wonderful and magical. Finally the paper was put to bed (that's finished in newspaper talk) and we all had to go to bed ourselves.

Luke smiled and said good night to both of us. I smiled at him. Carly smiled at him. Then we glared at each other.

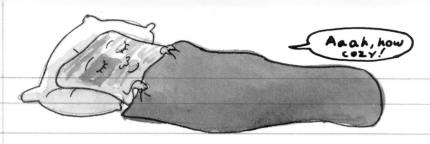

Aaah, how cozy!

I have a feeling ↑ only the newspaper slept well that night.

Carly and I didn't say anything as we walked back to our cabin until right before we got to the door. Then Carly exploded.

"How could you? You <u>know</u> I like Luke, we agree that it's okay that I like him, and then you go and flirt with him? What kind of friend ARE you?"

"Hey!" I snapped back. "I wasn't flirting — I was being friendly. I can't help it if Luke likes me. I didn't even think of him that way until <u>he</u> started flirting with <u>me</u>!"

"You are so full of it!" Carly's voice was hard and cold. "You like him — admit it! You like him!"

"Okay, I admit it." I tried not to yell. I didn't want the whole camp to hear us. "But I didn't <u>plan</u> on liking him. It just happened. It's not like I can turn my feelings off and on. And he did start it — not me. Besides, why can't we both like him?"

"Because we <u>can't</u>! Because that's not how friends treat each other. Because it's a betrayal!"

We stood outside the cabin, fighting in harsh whispers.

"I'm not betraying you! Can't we just leave it to Luke to pick who he likes more? I promise if he chooses you, I'll be fine with it. I'll still be your friend, no matter what." That's what I said, but I'm not sure I meant it. Anyway, I was certain Luke would choose me — we had so much in common, it was so easy to talk with each other. What would he and Carly talk about? It's true Carly was more cool than me. Maybe she was prettier — okay she _was_ prettier. But I was still confident that Luke liked me. I could just tell.

Okay, it's a deal then. We'll leave it up to Luke.

And we agree that we'll stay friends, no matter who he picks. No being a sore loser.

↑
Carly seemed just as sure that Luke liked _her_ best.

That got me thinking — how <u>do</u> you know if someone likes you? According to the movies, there are some obvious clues.

SIGNS OF A CRUSH

① Making moony goo-goo eyes at someone.

② Not being able to look someone in the face.

③ Stammering.

④ Laughing too long and too hard at someone's jokes.

⑤ Sending anonymous love notes.

⑥ Always managing to be near the person.

I'm not sure those are really accurate. They seem so Hollywood pat, so prepackaged and sugary. I think the hints are much more subtle and you have to be very observant to catch them. I have my own list of how to interpret body language.

Amelia's
SIGNS OF A CRUSH

He's not bored—
he's in love!

① A slightly flared nostril — the passion can't help but escape.

With just the tiniest hint of a smile.

② A raised eyebrow at just the right moment.

Add the moony eyes and it's totally obvious!

③ A smile that lasts a second too long.

Oops, didn't mean to bump you.

④ Accidentally on-purpose touching.

Standing a smidgeon closer than normal.

⑤ Standing a smidgeon closer than normal.

Nice job.

⑥ Casual-yet-on-purpose-with-no-apologies touching.

The next few days I tried to read Luke like a book to see if he really did like me. It was exhausting! Sometimes he'd smile at me a certain way and I'd <u>know</u> he liked me, but later I'd see him smile kind of the same way at Carly or Jeff or Mike. Then I didn't know what to think.

Once he touched my arm, but he did that to Luis too when they were working on page layout together. Then he winked at me one night by the campfire and I was sure that meant something until the next morning when I saw him wink at the hairnet lady in the cafeteria — obviously he doesn't have a crush on <u>her</u>.

You want some bacon with that, dahlin'?

Maybe a nice sausage or two?

Maybe he was just trying to be nice so he could get an extra portion of bacon or something. Or does he flirt with EVERYONE? I was beginning to wonder.

Who knew having a crush could be so tiring! What made it all the harder was that I didn't have Carly to talk to and get advice from. We weren't fighting anymore but that was because we were barely speaking to each other. It was terrible. She was right there, in the same cabin, on the same hikes, getting the same bug bites and blisters, singing the same camp songs but she might as well have been a million miles away. I saw her everyday and still I missed her.

We'd said we'd be friends no matter what.

But that wasn't what was happening.

It was strange. I began to look at Carly the same way I watched Luke, examining her for any sign that she wasn't mad at me anymore and was ready to be my friend again. Once she smiled and waved to me from the raft on the lake and I was so excited and happy until I realized she was waving to someone else.

I decided to talk to Carly about it. I wasn't so sure anymore about Luke, but I was certain about her — I knew we could be good friends. And I knew she liked me when we weren't both competing for the same boy.

"Carly," I said, "this is getting silly. We agreed we'd be friends no matter what, no matter who Luke picks, but we're not acting like friends."

"I'm not being unfriendly!" she snapped. "You're the one who's so standoffish."

"I am not!" I protested. "Or if I am, it's because you are."

"Well, that's a circular argument," Carly said.

She was right. We were like a dog chasing its tail. →

← We were going around and around in a circle, never getting anywhere.

"You're right," I admitted. "And I'm breaking the circle right now. I want us to be friends." I tried to soften my voice, to sound nice and warm. "So, what are you doing for your next column?"

The chill in Carly's eyes thawed. "Well," she began, "I'm thinking about doing a spoof on a gossip column, like camp romances, sightings of Bigfoot, that kind of thing."

"That sounds great," I said. And it did. Carly's full of good ideas. "I was going to do a comic on knot tying. There's something funny there, I'm just not sure what. Maybe how not to knot. Or all the funny knot names."

Carly nodded. It was such a relief to be talking with her again, to be normal with each other, the way we used to be.

We stood in the dark night, feeling better about each other, about everything. I didn't want to go into the light of the cabin and break the spell. Then we heard a rustling behind us. It was a skunk. At least it had a skunk's body and tail, but the head was stuck in a yogurt container. It couldn't see and was trying to shake off the container.

round
knot
↓

square
knot
↓

knotty
knot
↓

not
a
knot
↓

↑
Bigfoot—
never actually
seen.

↑
Camp Bear—
last sighted
in 1963.

Lake Ghost—
heard moaning
in 1972.
↓

We froze, staring at the skunk. I was afraid that if we startled it by making any noise, it would spray us. For once I didn't need a guide on how to read someone's expression — I could tell Carly was thinking the exact same thing.

"What should we do?" I whispered.

"We have to help it," she whispered back.

I like skunks. They have cute faces and nice, fluffy tails, but I don't like the disgusting stink they spray and I was pretty sure that getting sprayed close up would be UNBEARABLE. You'd have that musky smell inside your mouth, ears, nose — you'd breathe it deep inside your lungs. Maybe it wouldn't kill you, but it'd be MISERABLE.

But the skunk looked even more miserable, trying desperately to get the plastic carton off its head. And if we didn't help it, it would die.

I stopped thinking, I stopped smelling. I stopped breathing. I just stepped forward, grabbed the yogurt container, and quickly pulled it off. Then I braced myself, waiting for the awful spray.

I waited with my eyes closed tight, but no horrible smell came. I opened my eyes and saw the skunk amble off into the bushes, like a tame cat or dog, not a potentially highly stinky skunk.

Carly grabbed my arm, laughing. "Did you see that? It didn't even say thank you!"

"Oh yes, it did," I said. "It didn't spray us, did it? I can't believe I dared to take off that container."

"I can't believe it either." Carly grinned.

And just like that, we were friends again. We didn't say anything about Luke. We didn't need to.

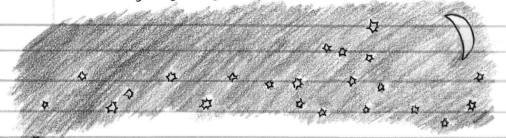

It was a beautiful night, crisp and clear. The stars sparkled in the sky and there was a new moon, pale and slender, a new beginning. It was so nice, I didn't even mind the bugs, the hard bunk bed, the smelly bathrooms, the dangerous skunks. I actually liked being at camp — for now. Which is good because there's still a couple weeks left to go.

That lasted a few days, until the dance was announced. Then Carly and I were right back where we started, wondering who Luke would pick, who he would ask to go to the dance with him.

CAMP RUNAMUCKA
DANCE-A-MUCKA!
IT'S THE LAST NIGHT OF CAMP - GO WILD!

Actually this time, things weren't as bad between us. We were still talking, even if a lot of the talk was teasing about how Luke would never choose the other person. The frosty anger was gone, melted away by the skunk. Instead there was a competitive edge — may the best girl win!

Carly thought that was her and sometimes I agreed with her. When she showed off at the lake, doing a perfect dive from the raft, I saw how Luke admired her. But I also saw how Luke liked my drawing, my sense of humor.

That's as important as graceful dives and strong swimming, isn't it? At least, I hope it is.

I always try to sit next to Luke at the campfires, but I've only managed to get a chance twice. He's sat next to Carly a couple of times too, but he's also been by Kayla, Leanne, and Sara. I wonder if that means anything.

I was coming back from the bathroom last night when I overheard Crystal and Jolene talking. I didn't mean to snoop, but I couldn't help listening.

It's so cute how they're all excited about this dance. It reminds me of when I was in middle school.

Yeah, I always had these intense crushes on guys who wouldn't look twice at me. Good thing I wised up.

I dunno — I kind of liked the whole impossibility of liking someone who barely knew I existed. It was so romantic.

Romantic or pathetic?

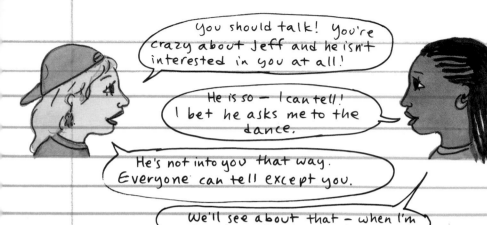

I had no idea that Jolene had a crush on Jeff! And I didn't know that grown women like her and Crystal had as much trouble telling if a guy likes them as Carly and I do. No wonder I'm so confused — even experts don't know. So much for all the helpful clues on how to read men. For some things, there are no maps. You just have to stumble around blindly and hope for the best.

The old daisy-plucking method was just as reliable.

I told Carly what the counselors said. After all,
we're in the same boat, clueless about who Luke
really likes better.

It was like old times. Carly curled up next to me
and we whispered together, trying not to wake
up anybody.

I do think he's going to ask me to the dance.

He almost did today, but then he got distracted by some kid from his cabin.

I mean, some things you know.

Or you think you know.

I thought for sure he was going to ask me today too. Then Kayla started talking to him.

Who's right? Are Carly's instincts better than mine?
Does anyone have a good sense about this stuff?
What if Jolene really doesn't get it? What if none
of us do? It's all a big mystery.

At least Carly and I can talk about this now. If
I'm wrong and Luke doesn't like me that way, I'll still
have Carly for a friend. I'll be sad and disappointed,
but I won't be lonely.

I almost forgot that Cleo's here. Camp's almost over and I hadn't seen her at all until today. She and some of the other counselors-in-training were decorating the cafeteria for the dance tomorrow. The theme is a Hawaiian luau even though we're in the mountains.

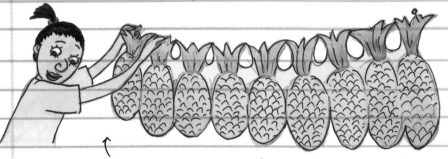

Cleo was hanging a banner of pineapples. She waved when she saw me.

"Hey, Amelia." Cleo sat next to me once she'd fixed her pineapples. "How are you liking camp? It's great, isn't it?"

"Yeah." I nodded. "It's good."

"You're going to the dance, aren't you? I'm going with Brendon." She nodded at a boy hanging paper parrots from the ceiling. "So who's y_o_ur boyfriend?"

"I don't have a boyfriend," I said. "I'm too young." I didn't want Cleo to know anything about Luke, but she was going to the dance too. She'd see everything.

"You don't need a date to go to the dance, you know," Cleo said. "Go anyway. It's gonna be a lot of fun. There's going to be a hula contest!"

I imagined Cleo wearing coconuts and a grass skirt. It wasn't a pretty picture.

Cleo, trying to be graceful...

...and keep the right rhythm at the same time - no easy task for her!

This dance was beginning to sound like the OPPOSITE of fun. Suddenly I didn't even want Luke to ask me because then I'd have to go and it would all be horribly embarrassing.

Cleo must have read my mind because she said, "Come on, Amelia, don't look like that! You don't have to hula-no one does. It's just to get into the spirit of things." She paused. "Don't worry, I'm not entering the hula contest. I promise I won't do anything to embarrass you."

"I'm not worried about that!" I lied. "It'll be great to see you at the dance."

"Good." Cleo nodded. "So what happened to Carly? Usually the two of you stick together but I saw her leave after dinner with some guy. So now she has a boyfriend?"

I could feel my cheeks get hot, though I tried not to blush. (Somehow trying not to look embarrassed only makes it worse.) "Luke's just a friend, not a boyfriend," I mumbled. "He's my friend too."

"Oh, I get it!" Cleo grinned. "You both like the same boy! That can be tough. I remember when that happened with Gigi and me. I swear, I almost clawed out that girl's eyes!"

I don't know why I thought Carly and I were the only friends with this problem. Of course this happened to other people. Of course friends survived this kind of thing all the time.

"So you and Gigi stayed friends?" I asked.

Yeah, we did. But she got the guy. I was sore for a while, but then I met someone else. And Gigi broke up with him anyway after a few weeks.

I mean, there's always another guy — no offense, Brendon — but there's only one Gigi! Guys come and go — she's forever.

I smiled. That sounded right. "Thanks, Cleo," I said and I meant it. For once I was glad she was around for me to talk to. She could even hula at the dance and I wouldn't mind.

I went to find Carly and told her what Cleo had said.

"Of course you'll always be my friend," Carly agreed. "But I have to tell you, I REALLY like Luke. I can tell you don't like him as much as I do, so why don't you just step out of the way? Isn't that what a true friend would do?"

I felt cornered. "How do YOU know how much I like Luke? Why should I bow out and not YOU? You're being so unfair — and selfish! You don't want a true friend — you want a doormat!"

It started out nice but it ended ugly. We were both furious and not speaking to each other — again.

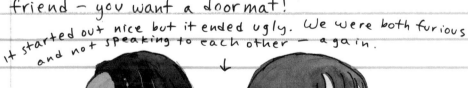

The next day was awful. Luke still hadn't asked me to the dance, but I could tell he hadn't asked Carly either. I decided to help him out a bit. Maybe he was just shy. I sat down next to him at lunch.

Don't the decorations for the dance look great? It's going to be a lot of fun.

Yeah, the cafeteria looks good and Hawaiian.

So will I see you at the dance?

Sure.

I waited for him to say more, to say "let's go together" or "want to come with me?" But he didn't. He just finished eating and said "See you later." See you later? That was it?

I put my head down on the table. It was time to admit that Luke would never ask me, that he didn't like me "that" way. Carly was right. He liked her better.

I heard someone sit down next to me. Had Luke come back? I looked up. It was Carly.

"You're right," she said. "He doesn't like me that way. He likes you. I'm sorry I yelled at you. I'm sorry I was such a selfish jerk." She sighed. "Have fun at the dance."

He hadn't asked Carly either? I shook my head. "Thanks for the apology, but Luke didn't ask me. I practically asked _him_, but he didn't take the hint."

Carly looked surprised. "Really?"

"Really," I said. "So how about we go to the dance together. And maybe Luke's just super shy and once he sees you there, he'll ask you to dance."

Carly rolled her eyes. "I'm not counting on that, but he might ask YOU. Either way, let's go and have fun."

I nodded. I have to admit that part of me was glad Luke hadn't asked Carly. That way I didn't feel so bad about him not asking me. Best of all, I had my friend back. Maybe no boyfriend, but still a best friend.

Hearts are complicated ← things. There's no explaining likes and dislikes, loves and hates.

When we got to the dance, Cleo was already there with Brendon, but there was no sign of Luke. Carly and I were eating cookies when we saw him walk in - WITH A DATE!

WITH KAYLA!

carly and I just stared at each other.

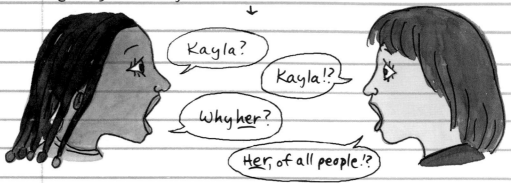

We were stunned, flabbergasted, floored, astonished. Kayla, the whiny, homesick kid? When did Luke ever say he liked her? When had we seen them together? When had all this happened?

I have to give Carly credit. At first she was in shock. Then she was furious. She waited until Kayla went to the bathroom. Then she stormed over to confront Luke.

"I thought you liked _me_," she said. "I thought you were going to ask _me_ to go with you."

Luke paled. "I do like you, Carly," he said, "but not _that_ way. I never said I did."

"Not with words, no, but in other ways!" Carly insisted.

I could see the steam coming out of Carly's ears. I actually felt sorry for Luke. He was right about Carly being strong. She could flatten him like a steamroller if she wanted to. She could bury him in an avalanche of angry words and we'd have to send a search party to dig him out. Carly fumed. Luke looked terrified. I held my breath.

"Your loss, then." Carly bit off the words. She didn't yell. She calmly turned around, walked over to Mike, and asked him to dance. That girl had style!

You would think that after that, the dance would be ruined. But it wasn't. It was fun. Carly and I danced a lot, with a bunch of different boys and with each other. Now that we knew who Luke really liked, all the tension was gone.

The funny thing was, I wasn't even jealous watching Kayla and Luke together. Maybe I would have been if it had been Carly and Luke, but just knowing that Luke chose someone like Kayla over someone like Carly... that made me like him a <u>lot</u> less.

I'm not saying Kayla was a bad person, but she was clearly a project, someone who needing tending, like a plant. Luke didn't pick ← her because of who she was, but because he could feel strong next to her, because he thought he could rescue her and make himself a hero.

Cleo came over to Carly and me at the end of the dance. "You guys look like you had a good time," she said.

"We did." I smiled. I hoped she wouldn't say anything about us liking the same boy. Sometimes Cleo can be sensitive. Luckily she was this time.

"Me too," she said instead. "If my best friend had been here, it would have been perfect."

Carly and I looked at each other. "Yeah," Carly said, putting her arm around me. "We're pretty lucky."

We walked back to our cabin, stopping to look at the stars. →

It was a beautiful night. We heard an owl hooting and saw a shooting star and there were no skunks. It was perfect.

"You know, Carly," I said, "we're too young to have a boyfriend anyway, don't you think? We have all of high school to deal with that. Maybe middle school should be a boyfriend-free zone."

"Maybe," Carly agreed. "But we aren't in school now. What about summers? Isn't camp supposed to be a place where you can try new things and if they don't turn out the way you expected them to, it doesn't really matter because it's camp, not regular life?"

"Yeah, that's a good thing about camp," I said.

I wondered what risky things I'd done this summer that I wouldn't have dared to try at home. Canoeing? Rock climbing? Freeing a skunk from a yogurt container? Practically asking a boy to a dance (or strongly hinting at least)? All those were things that could only happen at camp.

"Shhh." Carly hushed me. "Look," she whispered.

On the bench near our cabin there were two people sitting close together. Really close. So close they were kissing.

"Hey!" I whispered. "It's Jolene and Jeff!"

Carly nodded. "At least <u>she</u> was right about being liked."

I'll have to ask Jolene for <u>her</u> list of signs of a crush before we leave tomorrow. I'm glad to know <u>somebody</u> can get it right.

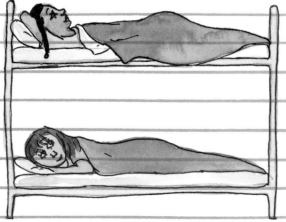

Finally, after <u>so</u> long, the bunk bed felt comfortable and cozy. Just in time to go home.

Amelia's Quick Guide to Surviving Summer Camp

① Send yourself a care package before you go — you'll be so happy to get it.

② Pack plenty of books. They're like portable friends.

③ Try everything at least once. Maybe you're good at archery and don't even know it.

SUMMER SURVIVAL CHECKLIST

Don't forget:

sunblock ↗

↑ sandals

↑ sunglasses

← summer fruit →

best friend
↓

Save some summer time for me!

MORE Amelia's Notebooks

write on! ↓

I've written ~~22~~ ~~23~~ 24 notebooks! which is your favorite?

Read on! ↓

The good, the bad, and the totally freaky! ↓

I wish I could *forget* them!

← Pssst! Did you hear the one about Mr. L?

Carly's favorite so far!

Plus all these from elementary school ↓

The first and original! →

↑ Still my favorite!

There's lots more info and fun stuff at marissamoss.com and KIDS.simonandschuster.com. Even a *real* Amelia movie!

Want more summer fun?
Look for my cousin Daphne's diaries. She's in 4th grade and FUNNY!
DAPHNE'S DIARY OF DAILY DISASTERS
The Name Game!
From the bestselling author of the Amelia series
MARISSA MOSS
DAPHNE'S DIARY OF DAILY DISASTERS
The Vampire Dare!
From the bestselling author of the Amelia series
MARISSA MOSS